Uncommitted Sin

By Craig Colboth

I0535600

This book is a work of fiction. Character names, places, business names and events are the work of the author's imagination and any resemblance to actual people, alive or dead, business establishments or locals are completely coincidental.

Chapter 1

George Kiel ran across the dirt road to his neighbor's farm. Blood stained his right sleeve; his left hand holding the wound. George's neighbor, Kenneth Lynch, was on his front porch when he saw his wounded neighbor running quickly for his assistance. "Ken, please help me! Rebecca shot me!" George screamed, "Please take me to my father's place, he can call the doctor." Kenneth threw the stick he was whittling on out to the yard, jumped off the porch and ran toward the barn. George waited for Kenneth to appear with his wagon. Before he could slow the wagon, George pulled himself up onto the seat.

"What the hell happened, George?" Ken asked as they started down the road. George paused and tried to collect his thoughts before he began to tell his story, "I do not know what happened, it was so fast. I was coming back from the barn when I heard a shot from the house. I ran to the kitchen door and saw Martha on the floor; blood was coming from her head. Rebecca was standing over her with a revolver. Before I could open my mouth she raised the revolver to me. I turned to run, but she got my arm. I ran to your place as quick as I could."

The men were quickly making their way to the farm of George's father, Charles Kiel. The farm was about two miles down the straight dirt road through Illinois corn fields. Less than a quarter mile from George's farm, they saw August Palmer, his hired hand tending to the crops. "August," George screamed as the wagon was swiftly moving by, "do not go to the farm. Rebecca has gone crazy, she shot me!" August did not know what to make of what just happened. As he saw the wagon disappear down the road, he decided to see what was wrong at the farm.

August jumped on his horse and rode swiftly to the house. "Misses Kiel? Are you okay?" August yelled as he rode toward the kitchen porch. He dismounted the horse, but heard nothing except bugs buzzing in the hot July air. With great caution he approached the house. As he stepped onto the kitchen porch, he again asked, "Misses Kiel, is everything okay?" There was nothing but the sounds of the bugs. He then peered into the kitchen through the dirty screen door.

On the floor laid Martha Vogal, Rebecca's mother and owner of the property. He could tell she was dead. He did not want to approach any further, but then he saw Rebecca. She was lying on the other side of the kitchen, blood streaming from her head and a revolver loosely lying in her right hand. He thought to step into the kitchen but promptly turned and fled to his horse. Believing the farm of Charles Kiel was where George and Kenneth were headed, he decided to ride there as well.

Charles Kiel was one of the wealthiest land owners in the whole area around Mill Grove. Charles was reaching an older age and was mostly retired from farm work, leaving it to his employees. He was in the parlor reading the days paper when he heard a wagon arrive in front of the house. Not expecting visitors, he got up from the chair with a groan to see who was there. Kenneth was helping George down from the wagon. "George, what happened?" Charles asked seeing the blood on his son's shirt. "Rebecca shot me! She shot Martha… she went crazy!" George cried.

Charles ran to the phone and rung the operator, "Sarah, call Doctor Wright, it's an emergency." Charles waited for the doctor to pick up his phone. Before the doctor could even say hello, Charles said with excitement "Its Charles Kiel. I need you at the farm right away. My son was shot in the arm… No I think it nicked him… Yes we will be waiting." Charles placed the receiver down only to pick it right back up and ring the operator again. "Sarah, call Deputy Johnson and tell him I need him at the farm immediately!"

As his father sat in the chair without expression, George told him what happened. Ken stood in the doorway nervously smoking while watching for the doctor and the deputy. The doctor arrived swiftly from town and ran to the house with a brown leather bag in hand. "Please let me see the wound George," Doctor Wright said as he carefully grabbed Georges arm. George took his left hand off of his arm to reveal a flesh wound.

"Well, she was not too good of a shot," Deputy Sheriff Alan Johnson dryly said as he walked through the door; his badge shining against his light gray uniform. Standing with him, panting like a heated dog, was August Palmer. "August stopped me on the road to tell me what happened," the deputy said. Before another word could be said August cried, "Misses Kiel is dead! So is Misses Vogal!" As the doctor cleaned his wound George wept softly then asked, "How can she be dead? What happened to her?" August took his straw hat off and wiped the sweat from his forehead, "I saw her lying on the floor, she shot herself…" George no longer wept and did not make any reaction as his father shook his head in disbelief.

"Doc, if it is fine with you, I want to take George back to his house. I need to know his story of what happened," Alan said. "Yes, he should be fine, but he needs some rest. George I will be by in the morning to check your wound," the doctor said as he was closing his bag. "Mister Lynch, did you see any of this happen?" Alan asked. "No Deputy, I was on the porch when George came running over asking for help." Ken said. "You did not hear anything?" Alan asked with a puzzled look on his face. Kenneth nervously took a puff off of his cigarette and exhaled a bluish-gray cloud of smoke, "No… no I did not hear a thing, sorry Deputy."

"Charles, please call the Glasford office and let Coroner Knight know what has happened and ask him to come out immediately. I will take George to the house," Alan said then looked to George, "Please come out to the automobile with me."

As they drove to the house George retold his story to the deputy. "I do not know what would cause her to do this, we were happy together. I thought we were happy…," George stated. As the car approached the house George asked, "Do I have to go inside? Do I… have to see them?" Alan stopped the automobile in the barn yard then looked at George, "No, you can stay here if you like. The coroner should be here at some point. I do not know if he will drive or take the streetcar to Mill Grove."

Alan entered the kitchen taking note of the scene. While they had only been dead for about one hour, the heat was taking to the bodies. A smell was starting and files were entering through a cut in the screen door. Alan knelt down next to Martha where he observed a small hole in her head behind her left ear. It appears that Rebecca came in from behind and shot her. Alan was new to the job, but came from Chicago and had seen murder before. Even with this knowledge, his stomach was turning from all of the blood on the floor.

He exited the kitchen and went back onto the porch to get air. "Is it true, is Rebecca dead?" George asked from the car. "Yes, but I have not

7

approached her body yet. I needed some air," Alan said while trying to breathe fresh, but thick humid air into his lungs. George looked forward out to the barnyard. He did not say a word nor cry when hearing the fate of his wife.

Alan reluctantly returned to the kitchen and with great care, stepped around Martha's body. Sitting between the women was the kitchen table. On it was cut apples that were turning brown in the heat. Next to them, flour was sprinkled and a ball of dough was about to be rolled out. Rebecca's body was on the floor close to one of the legs. She had her kitchen apron on with flour sprinkled on both it and her hands. "What would cause a woman to turn from making a pie to killing her mother and trying to kill her husband?" Alan said to himself. Then he saw the revolver in her right hand. He picked it up with his handkerchief and opened the chamber, four spent shells were found; two bullets remained. He looked at her face, her eyes were still opened. Her head was cocked slightly to the right and a single bullet hole was in her forehead above her right eye.

Alan took the gun with him out to the porch. As he placed the handkerchief wrapped gun on the porch railing, he looked toward his car to see George was gone. "George Kiel, where are you??" Alan yelled to barnyard. He did not hear a word, but then saw George sitting under the windmill. "I needed a drink, I need a real drink but I know there is nothing in the house," George stated. "Well, we can sit here and wait for the coroner…," Alan said,

"George, did you two have a fight today?" George looked down to the weeds growing next to the well head, "No, but we did have a quarrel last Friday. It was nothing really; I guess we seem to quarrel over stupid things; what she made for dinner, how long I spend in town… How I run the farm. I never thought she would do this, I mean, we may have a small fight, but always make up." Alan listened to the widow as he talked slowly, calmly. "Did you make up this time?" Alan asked bluntly. "No," George said with no hesitation.

The men rested under the windmill in the shade of the only tree in the barnyard. The air was hot with just enough of a breeze to make the windmill squeal as it tried to move while clouds seemed to be growing out of a distant wheat field. "Looks like a storm may be coming," George said, "I need to get that field taken care of. August and I were going to start harvesting it today." Alan wiped the sweat from his neck, "It's too hot to rain, too hot to do anything." As they looked to the field August Palmer arrived on his horse. "Deputy," August said, "the coroner asked that you meet him and a Doctor Richards in Mill Grove. They will be taking the street car from Glasford." Alan stood up and cracked his back, "George, I will take you back to your father's. When Coroner Knight is ready, I will come get you."

Deputy Johnson stood on the plank platform waiting for the streetcar. Sweat was running out from under his hat, but always the professional he would not remove it unless to tip it for any young woman that might walk by. Mill Grove was a small farming community that holds few businesses, most of which were to support the farms surrounding the town. However there was a library, three churches, an elementary school, a funeral home and on the outskirts, two taverns and a pool hall.

The electric street car line ran straight up main-street and was a branch line of a larger interurban line that ran from Chicago to Galena via Rockford and Freeport. Deputy Alan Johnson loved the small town and countryside he protected. While many of the youngsters of the town proclaimed they would leave when old enough to move to the busy cities, Alan was happy to leave Chicago. He was known to many of the town's people and he knew most of them, at least their names. Alan was starting to feel part of the community and no longer the city boy that many people labeled him as.

Alan reached for his pocket watch to see it was two-twenty. "The street car should be arriving at any time," Alan said to himself. As he waited, a large voice came from the side, "Deputy, how are you doing on this sweltering day?" Alan turned to see the town's mayor Roy Hines and his wife Nancy, who was better known as the town's busybody.

"Oh, I am doing well Mayor. Hello Misses Hines," Alan stated while tipping his hat.

Before the mayor could get another word out, Nancy said with a tone of urgency, "I heard that there may have been some kind of trouble this morning on the Vogal farm?" Alan cleared his throat, "I had to go out there but I cannot comment about what transpired." Alan looked down the track to see the headlight of the street car. "Well, I was just wondering…," Nancy tried to say as the mayor stopped her with a look of displeasure.

The street car was slowing to the platform with the brakes squealing as they tried to stop the older wooden car; its glossy orange paint shining in the sun. Alan watched the car stop then looked to the elderly couple. "Misses Hines, please let Sarah down at the exchange know that she is only to be connecting the circuits, not listening in'" Alan said humorously.

Coroner Knight stepped off of the car and with him was a tall quiet man that Alan did not know. "Deputy Johnson, this is Doctor Richards, he will be assisting me," Coroner Knight stated. The doctor pulled out a cigarette from his tin and lit it. "Please to meet you Deputy," the doctor said. "Deputy, we should notify the undertaker to be ready to assist when I am ready," the coroner stated. "We can stop on the way to the farm," Alan said while staring at the odd doctor. As the men walked to Alan's car, the motorman hit the gong two times and street car started to move as the traction motors roared to life with little effort. "They need to work on the tracks out here, I think I may have cracked a rib," Doctor Richards joked while smoke blew out of his nose.

After making a quick stop at the Koonze and Haske Funeral Parlor, the men continued to the murder scene. The coroner was taking note of the skies that were darkening while the wind was picking up. After a few short minutes they pulled into the barn yard of Vogal farm. August Palmer was taking the cows into the barn anticipating the coming storm.

"Coroner, the bodies are in the kitchen through that door on the small porch," Alan said while pointing to the weather-beaten farm house. As the men walked to the house, the windmill was turning faster and thunder was in the distance. "I guess we made it in time for a storm," the coroner stated. The doctor simply coughed in agreement. "Coroner, the revolver is on the porch railing in my handkerchief. I took it from Misses Kiel's hand," Alan stated. "Why would you do that? It's not like she would be able to use it again," Doctor Richards laughed. "I do not know… I guess it was the right thing to do," Alan said trying to decide if the good doctor was taking a shot at him.

"Deputy, please tell me who we are looking at and what you believed happened," the Coroner said. Alan did his best to ignore the smell that was becoming stronger by the minute, "Right before you is Misses Marta Vogal. She is the mother of Rebecca and the owner of the farm. Over there is Misses Rebecca Kiel. From what George Kiel stated, he was in the barnyard and heard a shot. He came to the door and saw Martha on the floor bleeding. He looked up and saw Rebecca with the revolver. He turned to run causing her to take a shot at him, grazing his right arm. He then ran to the neighbor across the road for help."

The corner looked around the kitchen. "Well, the bodies do appear to tell the same story. I am guessing after she took the shot at her husband, she turned the gun on herself," the coroner stated. "Doctor, let us examine the bodies, but I think this is a simple murder-suicide," the coroner proclaimed feeling as if the trip was nothing more than a waste of time.

Lightning flashed in the sky with a thunderous canon like roar of thunder quickly following. As the Deputy stood by the door watching the storm, the men examined the bodies. Alan was thinking to himself that in Chicago they would treat this as more than a simple murder-suicide, but he had no power to intervene in the coroner's investigation. In less than twenty minutes both the storm and coroner were finished. "Deputy after you take us back to the street car, please let the undertaker know that they can take the bodies, there is nothing more for me to do," Coroner Knight stated.

"Coroner... does this not look odd to you?" Alan asked. "How do you mean?" the coroner asked with a stressed tone. "Look at the table," Alan started, "why would she go through the trouble of cutting apples and making dough only to go kill her mother and herself? Doesn't that seem odd?" The men stood speechless for a few seconds until Doctor Richards said, "Well, maybe she was mentally unstable, cut too many apples in her life."

Corner Knight ran his left hand through his damp hair then said, "Deputy Johnson, I will take my notes and the gun to a coroner's jury tonight. If they think there is more to this, they will vote to keep the case open. However as I see it, Rebecca killed her mother, tried to kill her husband and then turned the gun on herself." Alan tired not to show his disbelief, "Would you at least like to talk with George Kiel before you go?" The coroner looked to the bodies and said, "No, I do not see a need to put him through any more pain."

The men returned to town on the now muddy road. The sun was back out brightly and the humidity was worse than before. Alan got the men to the platform just as the street car arrived for its return trip to Glasford. "Deputy, I will let you know in the morning what the jury found," Coroner Knight stated. The men stepped onto the street car just in time for the motorman to start the trip back to Glasford.

Alan watched the streetcar leave and then returned to his car. A few moments later he stopped to notify the undertakers that they could remove the bodies and then proceeded to the farm of Charles Kiel.

George and Charles were sitting in rocking chairs on the front porch of the house as Alan approached. "George, the coroner feels what you said is the how the events played out and that Rebecca turned the gun on herself after trying to kill you., Alan stated while wiping the sweat off his forehead.

"You do not believe what my son said, Deputy??" Charles asked in an angered tone. "I believe your son sir, but I have a job to do and I do it fully," Alan said with a stern tone, "They will be holding a coroners inquiry tonight in Glasford. We should know in the morning what they have found. The undertaker will be picking up Rebecca and Misses Vogal shortly. You should contact them about what arrangements you want, good night gentlemen." Alan left the men to sit on the porch and morn their losses as he left for Mill Grove.

Alan arrived in town just in time to see August Palmer about to enter The Rock Wall, one of the town's two taverns. "August, can I talk with you for a few minutes?" Alan asked from his car. August walked over, still looking green from the day's events. "August, have you ever seen Mister Kiel and his wife fight?" Alan asked. "I think you would be better to ask if I never saw them fight," August said, "They fought a lot, I never saw him hit her, but George is a mean man. He is the black sheep of his family. I mean look at his father and brothers. All are rich land owners, well liked in the community, but George is not that bright. The only reason he has that farm is because he married Rebecca. That farm was her fathers; when he died, her mother took over. When Rebecca got married, he ran the farm, but Misses Vogal still owns it… Did own it."

"Why where you out checking the corn this morning? George stated that you two were going to harvest the wheat today," Alan said. "I told him we needed to harvest the wheat, but he told me to go check the corn, make sure it is growing properly, like he would really know," August barked back with an angered tone.

"Deputy there is something you should know, but I did not want to tell you in front of George or his father. Not long ago, Misses Kiel asked me to hide George's revolver from him. She was afraid that he might use it on her," August said, "when you were in the house with the coroner I was in the barn where I sleep. His gun is still where I hid it… but my revolver is missing."

Alan looked at August with a queer look, "Are you quite sure of this August?" August looked around to see some of the locals listening to the conversation, "Yes, quite sure Deputy…" Alan

16

noticed the observers then said, "I will talk with you tomorrow August, I need to make a phone call."

Alan swiftly drove to his office. Once inside he picked up the telephone receiver and turned the magneto handle three times. "Hello deputy, who do you need?" came a voice over the ear piece. "Sarah please get me Coroner Knight," Alan stated firmly. "I cannot Deputy, the storm took down a few poles leading to Glasford, the lineman hopes to have it fixed by the morning, is there anyone else I can get for you?" she asked. "No," Alan said disappointed, "Say, what time is the last street car to Glasford?" There was a short pause then Sarah stated. "Sorry, you missed it, it was seven o'clock. It is fifteen minutes past" Alan looked to the wall clock then said, "Thank you Sarah." Alan appeared to be deep in thought while he slowly hung up the ear piece.

Chapter 2

Richard Koonze & James Haske were the town's undertakers who ran their business out of a large Victorian house on Main Street. The men were well known since they were the only undertakers outside of Glasford in all of Park County.

Richard and James arrived at the Vogal house about eight o'clock on the night of the incident. Their job was a gruesome one, but they did it with dignity. They first placed Martha into a pine casket. Next they went to move Rebecca. James being the larger of the two men picked up Rebecca by the shoulders while Richard had her feet. As they were moving Rebecca, James noticed more blood running from her head. "Richard, let's put her down, I think I see something" James said. They placed her on the floor where he could get a closer look.

James turned her head to reveal a hole behind her left ear. "It must be where the bullet exited," Richard stated. "I don't know, don't you think the hole would be bigger? It looks like the same size as the hole in her temple," James said with an inquisitive tone. "Well in any case, you would think that Coroner Knight would have found that and noted it if it was something," Richard said, "come on let's get her in the box, Charles Kiel said he wants them buried tomorrow afternoon."

"It does not seem right that they will not have a proper funeral or anything like that, just placed in the ground with a few words," James said with a somber tone. "Is that your mind speaking or your balance sheet?" Richard chuckled. James shook his head in disbelief at what his partner just stated.

The men loaded the caskets onto their cart and placed a blanket on top. As they made their way to town, they passed Charles Kiel's farm. "Do you think we should stop and ask if they have any further wishes?" James asked. "No, Charles was clear. He said would contact Saint James church and have two plots ready for the morning. Misses Vogal's husband is buried there," Richard said.

"I am going to talk with Deputy Johnson in the morning…. about the second hole we found," James said determined. "James, if you wish, but I am sure the coroner already knows about it," Richard stated bluntly. They sat quietly the rest of the way to town. As they pasted the tall stalks of corn, the sun slowly set into a purple haze on the horizon.

The next morning, the phone rang in the office of the funeral home. James picked up the phone, then calmly, sincerely and with a slight monotone said, "Koonze and Haske funeral home, how may I help you?" An angered tone fired back over the line, "This is Charles Kiel. There has been a change in plans. Saint John's Lutheran Church will not allow Rebecca to be buried in their grave yard."

19

James asked puzzled, "Why? What reason would they not allow this?" Charles' voice grew tenser, "It is because Rebecca killed herself. They consider that a sin and said they will not allow a sinner to be buried in their grave yard."

"Well, I can make other arrangements Mister Kiel," James said reassuringly. "I already have. Rebecca will be buried in Mount Elm cemetery. I already talked to the owner; he said a plot will be dug by this afternoon. Martha will be buried as planned at Saint Johns," Charles barked. "Yes sir, do you want a grave side mass for both of them?" James asked already knowing the answer. "No! They will be buried and that's it. My son cannot continue to feel his pain from what that woman… Rebecca did," Charles stated dryly. "I will make sure all of this is done as you wish," James said. He barely got the words out as he heard the phone click off.

James hung up the receiver, then picked it back up and turned the crank a few times. "Sarah, please get me Deputy Johnson," James asked. After a short pause, "Deputy Johnson" came over the line. "Deputy, this is James Haske. I need to talk with you. It has to do with the murders yesterday," James said in a soft tone. "Okay, I will be right over James," Alan said. "Thank you, deputy," James said then hung up. Alan thought for a moment, then hung up the receiver and put on his hat. It was a short two block walk to the funeral home. He opened the wrought iron gate and proceeded up the walkway to the painted porch. As he raised his hand to knock on the door, it opened with James' assistance.

"Hello James, you sounded odd on the phone. Is everything well?" Alan asked. "Deputy, when Richard and I were placing Rebecca into the casket last night, I noticed something odd. Now, Coroner Knight may already know, so I might just be telling you something you already know...," James said unassured of what he may be doing. As James was talking, the phone rang a few times. "Well, what did you find?" Alan asked. "Rebecca had what looks like a second bullet hole. It is behind her ear," James said pointing to the same area on his head. "Are you sure, can I see her?" Alan asked. "Yes Deputy I am sure of it, I saw it in my mind all night. Please follow me I will take you to her," James said.

"Come with me to the staging room, it is where the departed wait for their final journey," James said with a queer tone. The men could hear the sound of nails being pounded as they approached the small room at the rear of the house. As the men walked into the room, Richard just finished sealing Rebecca's coffin. "Richard, the deputy would like to see Rebecca," James said. "Sorry deputy, but the casket is sealed," Richard said while glaring at James. "Richard, I need to see this second hole," Alan said in cross way. "I am sorry deputy that was the coroner on the phone. The jury came back with their judgment at two o'clock this morning. Murder-Suicide. The case is closed," Richard said firmly, "I am sorry Deputy, but I do not have to show you anything. Besides the cart is waiting to take them to the cemetery."

"Wait, the phone lines were down to Glasford, Sarah said they would not be fixed until sometime this morning," Alan said in a puzzled tone. "Well they must have got them fixed last night Deputy. Now, if you would please let us get back to work," Richard said. "Yes, I will be going now. I think I have a phone call to make," Alan said while passing through the back door to the outside.

Alan ran not to his office, but to the phone exchange above the drug store. He ran up the stairs then opened the door to the small room. One half held banks of glass cased batteries and mazes of wires, the other the switch board. Sitting in front of it, day dreaming out the window was Sarah, the operator. "Sarah… Sarah!" Alan said to get her attention. She turned with a startled look that quickly changed when she laid eyes on Alan. Sarah was the old maid type; her red hair tied up tight. She wore no makeup and had no glamour. Sarah had never married, but always dreamed of finding her husband. She also held a secret crush on Alan and hoped that he would need a call placed.

"Sarah, you said that the lines were down to Glasford," Alan stated without a single breath. "Yes Deputy, they were. The lineman called me about six o'clock stating the lines were repaired," Sarah said with a slightly flirtatious tone. "Did a call come through from Glasford for the funeral home?" Alan asked. "Yes, about fifteen minutes ago… Murder-suicide… I mean, that is what I heard on the street this morning," Sarah said while trying to pull the words back into her mouth. "Sarah, I need to place a call to the coroner right now," Alan said. "Yes Deputy, you can use the phone behind you. I will patch you in." Sarah said with a smile.

Sarah turned to the board, pulled a cord from the desk and placed it into one of the jacks. She then turned the handle in two quick bursts. "Glasford, please place a call to the coroner's office, yes I will hold," Sarah said then paused until she heard someone on the other end of the line, "Coroner Knight, please hold for a call from Deputy Johnson". Sarah pulled another cord from the desk and placed it into one of the many jacks on the board. "Deputy, you can pick up now." Sarah said.

"Coroner Knight, this is Deputy Johnson. Is it true the jury found this a murder-suicide?" Alan asked. "Yes deputy, we were up late last night, well really this morning. They had no other choice. There was no evidence coming to a different conclusion," the coroner said while yawning. "Coroner, I have the evidence, well, I believe I have some evidence," Alan said. "What evidence?" the coroner asked. "I cannot say on this line coroner, please come here quickly. You may also want to bring States Attorney Lange," Alan said.

"I cannot ask the state's attorney to come out for evidence that I do not even know exists!" the coroner barked back, "Besides he is out kissing babies or whatever candidates up for reelection do." Alan did his best to remain calm. "Please coroner, I will have evidence for you, but we will need the state's attorney for the rest," Alan said defiant. "Very well deputy, but you better have something good, or it will be both of our necks on the block. If I can convince him to come, we will be there shortly," the coroner said with an annoyed tone then a final deep yawn.

Alan hung up the phone, "Thank you Sarah." The operator removed her headphones and smiled, "Oh, I am here to help Deputy. What were you talking about with the coroner?" Alan backed to the door leading out of the room, "I cannot say Sarah, but I am sure you will find out in due time." Alan tipped his hat to the love starved woman and walked down the stairs.

Deputy Johnson left the exchange and quickly ran to his office to get his car. He drove out to the farm of George Kiel going through patches of fog rolling out of the fields. Passing Charles' farm, it appeared as nothing happened the day before; it was just a normal day on the farm. Alan arrived at the farm to see the cows were out in the pasture enjoying the morning's load of hay. The wheat field was as it was the day before, untouched and turning a further golden brown.

Alan got out and approached the barn. The main door was open allowing the cool, fresh air in. "August, are you here?" Alan asked. "Just a minute deputy, I will be right there," August said then climbed down from one of the lofts. His overalls were covered in grain dust and sweat was rolling from his head and back. "August, I need for you to get dressed and come with me to my office," Alan said sternly. "Deputy, I have work to get done, George will fire me...," August said wiping the sweat from his head with a dirty rag. "Please, I need for you to tell me everything you know. Coroner Knight and States Attorney Lange will be meeting us," Alan said with haste.

"Deputy, I want to help, but I cannot lose my job...," August said with a worried tone. "August, you do not understand, I think George killed Rebecca and Martha. I need your help!" Alan exclaimed while trying to contain his anger. "If you need my help deputy, I will get dressed, but if George asked where I was, what do I tell him?" August asked. "You can tell him I needed your assistance," Alan said relieved knowing that his greatest piece of evidence so far will be coming with.

After a few minutes, August was washed up and dressed in clean, but still ragged work clothes. They were getting into the car when Alan asked, "Have you talked with George this morning?" August was looking into a small rectangular mirror combing his hair and said, "No, I do not think he

25

has been back since yesterday." The men drove back
to town taking the long way to avoid going past
Charles Kiel's farm. They arrived just in time for the
street car carrying the coroner and states attorney to
arrive at the platform with its signature squeal. After
a brief introduction, the men walked to Alan's office
trying to stay in the shade of the buildings.

Alan's office was not more than a large
room with a single jail cell in the corner. The only
furniture was his desk and chair. A few other chairs
sat along the wall, full of dust as there was no need
for them. A picture of Sheriff Bonner hung on the
wall to the right and slightly below a picture of
President Taft.

"Gentlemen, please sit down," Alan said to
the coroner and states attorney. They dusted the
chairs with their handkerchiefs not wanting to get
their suits dirty. "August, please sit in my chair.
Gentlemen, this is August Palmer. He is George
Kiel's hired hand. August, please tell us about
George's gun," Alan said while standing at the side
of the desk like an attorney cross-examining a
witness.

August had a scared look on his face as if
he was the one in front of the confessor. "Well...
about a month ago Rebecca, um, Misses Kiel asked
for me to hide George's revolver. She said she was
afraid that George would kill her with it," August
said with a nervous tone, "Yesterday, while the
deputy and the coroner were in the house. I went to

where I hid his gun in the barn. I hid it on a rafter tie close to the peak of the roof. It was still there. I then went to my room in the barn… I have this small room at the end of the stalls. I own a revolver that I keep in the drawer of a small desk I have. I went to check it and it was gone. I have never used it except to shoot at rats or crows."

"August, did George know you had a gun?" Lange asked. "Yes sir, he knew," August said. "Did Misses Kiel know you had a gun?" Lange asked. August thought for a moment then answered, "Yes, I believe so. I mean, I never outright told her, but I am sure she knew, everyone out here has a gun or two."

"August, please describe your gun," Alan asked. "It's dark gray with a polished wood handle. It is a twenty-two caliber," August said. Alan looked at Lange, "That describes the gun I found in Rebecca's hand. August, please tell us about the relationship between the Kiel's."

August felt a little uncomfortable at the question asked of him, "They fought a lot. They fought almost every day. Misses Vogal did not approve of the way George ran the farm and that caused many fights also." August stopped what he was stating and looked out the window to the dusty street. "August, did any of the fights turn physical?" Lange asked. "No sir, at least not in front of me. I would not tolerate that. I would have shot him myself if I saw him raise a hand to Rebecca," August said strongly. "August, how old are you?" Lange asked. "I am twenty-nine sir," August retorted with little ease.

"Did you have any feelings toward Misses Kiel?" Lange asked. "No sir, she is a good woman… was a good woman. I would do anything for her, but no I did not have romantic feelings for her," August said while holding his head down.

"Coroner, how old was Misses Kiel?" Lange asked. "Thirty-two" the coroner replied after popping up from a quick nap. "How old is Mister Kiel?" Lange asked. "About forty I believe," the coroner replied. "August, you were much closer in age to Misses Kiel than her husband was. Did it appear to you that could have been a problem to Mister Kiel?" Lange asked.

"No, I do not think so sir," August said. "How was it you came to work for Mister Kiel?" Lange asked while he crossed his arms. "I actually did not work for Mister Kiel; I work for and was paid by Misses Vogel," August said feeling as if he was being interrogated. "Did Mister Kiel feel angered by your employment?" Lange asked with a slightly louder tone. "I do not believe so," August said.

"I assume you ate with the family. When you ate with them, did Misses Kiel ever show you better treatment than she did to her husband?" Lange asked. "Yes I ate with them and yes sometimes, I mean, she would ask me if I wanted seconds or thirds…," August said feeling uneasy again. "Did she ask her husband for extra portions?" Lange asked. "No, he normally would take a mound of food and when he was done, he would leave the table," August said with his tone getting tense.

"Did you ever spend time with Misses Kiel when her husband or mother were not present?" Lange asked. "Yes, if she had chores for me to do…" August said looking out of the window again. "I want to ask you again, where you involved with Misses Kiel?" Lange barked. "No, I was not. I wanted to be… but she was faithful…," August said with a somber, quiet tone. "Did you ever ask her… talk with her in a romantic way?" Lange asked with a persistent tone. August could feel his grief turning to anger, "Yes, but she would not respond. Not the way I hoped!"

"Mr. Lange, is this line of questioning leading to anything? Alan asked. "Deputy, are you this man's attorney?" Lange snapped back. "No," Alan responded. "Well if this man is your evidence, we need to know not just what he says, but everything that has happened in the past that evolves him and this family," Lange stated sternly.

August was looking out of the window as the men fought over his testimony. "Now August, where were you during the shooting?" Lange asked. "I was out in the north field, checking the corn," August said with a trance like tone not taking his mind off of the dusty street. "Is this a normal responsibility for you?" Lange asked getting annoyed by the farm hand's daydreaming. August turned to Lange, "Yes, but George specifically asked that I check on the corn from that field."

"How far were you from the farm house?" Lange asked. "About a quarter of a mile, maybe a little further I guess," August said. "Did you hear the shots?" Lange asked. "No sir… Didn't know nothing happened until George went by with Kenneth Lynch. Ken was taking George to his father's house. George yelled to me to stay away from the house… said Rebecca was shooting and tried to kill him," August said trying not to show his growing anger.

"What did you do at that moment?" Lange asked. "I jumped on my horse and rode back to the house as quick as I could," August said softly. "Why did you not stay away? Where you not afraid of being shot?" Lange asked. "I don't know… I mean… Rebecca would never shoot anyone. She would not hurt anyone. I was not afraid of her… I was more afraid of what he may have done to her," August said trying to hold his tears back.

"August… please be honest with me. Did you have anything to do with the attempted murder of George Kiel or the murders of Rebecca Kiel and Martha Vogal?" Lange asked sternly. August's grief and sadness flashed over to anger in a heartbeat, "No! I swear I did not. I loved Rebecca... I would never hurt her…" August broke down in tears and sob uncontrollably. Alan walked over and placed his hand on August's shoulder to comfort him. "August why don't you go out and get some air, I want to talk with the men alone for a few minutes," Alan said. August got up, wiped the tears from his face and walked out onto the sidewalk without saying another word.

"Well Deputy... I believe him, but that is not enough to reopen this case. Any Judge would throw me in the pen if I brought this little to him," Lange said. "Mister Lange, there is one more piece of evidence, but I need your help to get it," Alan said.

"What is that?" Lange asked as he straightened up in his chair. "James Haske the undertaker found a second bullet hole on Misses Kiel's skull," Alan said. "Where?" Coroner Knight asked sternly. "Behind her left ear, like that of Misses Vogal," Alan stated with little pride. "Coroner, did you note a second wound?" Coroner Knight looked off toward Alan, "No, I did not. How do you know it is not an exit wound?" Alan now felt under the gun like August, "According to James, it is the same size as the hole in her temple. Also, there are four bullets missing from the gun. George stated she fired once at him. By my count that means we have one bullet unaccounted for."

"Mr. Lange, I need your help to get the body returned back to the coroner's custody," Alan stated. "Where is the body?" Lange asked after a deep sigh. "More than likely, she is being buried right now," Alan replied quietly. Lange's face turned red with Alan's statement. "Listen, I will need to go to Judge Hollingshead in Glasford," Lange said, "it will be risky, but I will tell him what we have. If I'm lucky he will not laugh me out of his chambers. Deputy, tell me straight, do you really think this is anything other than suicide?"

Alan held his ground firmly, "I think there is enough here to believe that Rebecca Kiel did not shoot herself. I cannot say what else happened in that kitchen, but I firmly believe she did not kill herself."

"Well Coroner Knight, we need to get back to Glasford. I will file a motion with Judge Hollingshead as soon as we return," Lange said, "Deputy… we will be in touch. Do me a favor and please keep an ear to any rumors going through town. You never know, it may be some help to us."

Lange and Knight stood up with Lange making sure to dust off the seat of his pants. The men proceed to the door when Lange turned and looked back toward Alan. "Deputy", he said, "you better be right about this." Alan gave a half smile, "Do not worry… I am." The men left the office and walked out onto the wooden sidewalk passing August as if he was not there.

The men made their way back toward the streetcar platform when a small boy stopped them, "Excuse me, would either of you like to buy a newspaper?" Lange looked down to him and with a smile said, "Yes, I'll take one son." He handed the boy a nickel who in return gave him one of the papers held under his arm. Lange unfolded the paper to see the headline in bold print: 'MURDER HITS KIEL FAMILY. CHARLES KIEL'S DAUGHTER IN LAW KILLS MOTHER, SELF'

Lange showed the headline to Knight and sighed, "I do not know if opening this case is the right thing to do." Coroner Knight looked down the street to see the street car coming, "I trust Deputy Johnson… even if it makes me look incompetent." Lange looked at him with a slight detest and stated, "You're not up for reelection…"

Chapter 3

States attorney Lange was sitting in his office when the phone rang. "Lange here," he barked with his usual tone of displeasure. "Lange, this is Hollingshead. I want you and Knight in my office in five minutes," came the voice over the phone. "Yes sir," Lange replied feeling his stomach tighten. Lange placed the receiver down only to pick it right back to call Coroner Knight, "Hollingshead wants us in his office in five minutes." Coroner Knight acknowledge with a grunt only to show his own discomfort.

The men walked to the doors of Judge Hollingshead's chambers. "Are you ready?" Lange asked. Knight just rolled his eyes then reached to knock on the door. "Come in!" was the swift reply. Judge William Hollingshead was known as one of the strictest judges outside of Chicago. He was also known as being honest. This is the reason Lange wanted him to decide if they could exhume Rebecca's body. Other judges in the county were known as being friends with the richer members of the community. However Hollingshead was more known for not just turning down brides, but making examples of those who thought money could influence his decisions.

"Mr. Lange I read your motion to exhume the body of Rebecca Kiel. I also read the evidence you have to ask for this motion. Now, you do know that if you do not find what you are looking for, you could be opening this county up to a very large lawsuit," the judge stated. "Yes your honor," Lange replied like a scolded child. "Coroner Knight, you did not see a second wound on the body, why is that?" the judge asked. "Well your honor, I did not see it, I did not think under the conditions there would be a second wound…," Knight replied with his own uneasiness.

"Coroner, is it not your job to find the evidence to come to a conclusion… not just jump to a conclusion because of how it appears the body looks?" the judge preached in a sharp tone. "Yes your honor, I should have looked more carefully at the body," Knight replied. "What is worse is that a simple undertaker did your job better than you!" the judge retorted heatedly.

"Gentlemen, I will allow you to exhume the body, but you must notify George Kiel of the fact you are doing this. You will also allow him to have consul with him during the exhumation of the body. Should you find the evidence you need, you will need to reconvene the coroner's jury to rule as if this was double murder," the judge stated as he pulled a piece of paper out of his desk drawer.

"By signing this you will have the authority to exhume Misses Kiel's body. I want to know what you find the minute you two return to town," the judge said as he dipped his pen into a bottle of black ink and then signed the paper. "I will bring you the results as soon as we can your honor," Lange said with a relieved tone to his voice.

After they thanked the judge, the men swiftly left his office for the safety of the hallway. "You should feel good Ben, you still have a job," Lange said to the coroner, "I will be heading right out to Mill Grove to serve the papers. Be ready to be at the grave yard early tomorrow morning." The coroner just shook his head with disbelief, "I'll be ready... don't worry, I will be ready. I hope we are not disturbing that body for no reason..."

Alan was sitting at his desk watching fly's buzz in and out of the windows of the office. A brass electric fan sitting on his desk moved the heavy, hot air around but really did little to cool the room. Suddenly the door swung open and States Attorney Lange rushed in to pronounce the news. "Deputy, let's get out to Charles Kiel's farm to serve the papers," Lange said, "I want the body exhumed first thing in the morning before it gets too hot."

Alan looked at the husky with surprise. "Well?" Lange asked, "What are you waiting for?" Alan took a deep breath then said, "Well... I guess you can say I am a little surprised." Lange walked over to the wall, picked up Alan's hat and placed it on the desk in front of Alan. "You'll need that... let's get moving," Lange said dryly.

The men got in Alan's car for the short drive to the farm. Alan observed that the few people out on the streets were taking note of the suited stranger in town. He wondered if word would reach George before they did. They pulled into the gravel driveway of Charles' farm to see his workers busy with the daily chores. As they got out of the car, Charles walked out onto the porch, his weathered skin prominently showed his displeasure. "Mister Kiel, I am States Attorney Lange, is George here?" the stout man said, his suit showing stains of sweat. "He's inside… George come out here," Charles yelled to the house then turned to spit chewing tobacco onto the ground near Alan's feet.

George walked out of the front door onto the wood porch. His arm was bandaged where the bullet nicked it; he was unshaven and his clothes looked as if he had slept in them. "George, this here is the state's attorney, he would like to speak with you," Charles said while dipping into his tobacco tin. "George Kiel, this is an order from the Honorable William Hollingshead giving us permission to exhume the body of your wife Rebecca tomorrow morning," Lange stated then handed the paper to George.

"What is this all about?" Charles demanded. "Sir, we have reason to believe that Rebecca did not take her own life. You do have the right to have consul present during the exhumation and George you must be present," Lange replied. "Oh, I will have a lawyer there… maybe more than one!"

Charles barked to Lange. "That is your right sir," Lange replied, "good night gentlemen; we will see you in the morning." Charles ripped the paper from George's hand and shook his head in disbelief as he read it. Lange and Alan walked to the car that was parked in the shade of a willow tree. "Deputy, please take me to the grave yard," Lange said. "We'll be there shortly. It's not far," Alan said as he went to crank the car over.

The Mount Elm cemetery was a ten minute drive from the Kiel farm. It was a simple square yard on the side of the road. Corn fields surrounded it on the other three sides. Brick columns about four feet tall were at the corners and on either side of the main gates with wrought iron fences in-filling between the columns. Over the gate was a hanging sign that said 'Mount Elm Cemetery.' The gate was closed for the night already, but they walked up to it to see the place were Rebecca was laid to rest.

Under an elm tree was a mound of dirt with a simple wooden cross placed at the far end. "There she is," Alan said. Lange looked at the mount of earth quietly for a few seconds. "Deputy, are you the only officer in this area?" Lange asked. "Yes, but I can call in deputies from other parts of the county if needed," Alan said. "Please keep a man at this grave yard until tomorrow. I do not trust the Kiel's," Lange replied. "I will stay here personally," Alan said.

The men left the cemetery and drove back to Mill Grove. The breeze was causing the corn stalks to rustle under the sky turning amber red from the setting sun. When they arrived at Alan's office, sitting on a bench in front of the office was a young woman. She was wearing a blue dress with a white top. Her long dark hair was laying down her back and firmly in her left hand was a small red book. As they approached, the woman stood from the bench,

"Miss Lynch what are you doing here this late?" Alan asked with curiosity. "I have something you might want to see," the young woman said. "Robin, this is Mister Lange; he is the state's attorney from Glasford. This is Robin Lynch, Kenneth Lynch's youngest daughter," Alan said. Robin looked around to see that no one else was within hearing range, "Deputy, I heard that you believe Rebecca was murdered." Lange chuckled, "News does travel quickly in this town." Alan gave a queer look and said, "Miss Lynch, you should not be out this late on your own, where are your parents?"

"They are out visiting, my father would be angry if he knew I was here talking with you about this. Deputy, this is Rebecca's diary," Robin said while giving the book to Alan, "she gave it to me to hold for her. She would take it to write in, but asked that I keep it safe otherwise. She said she feared that her husband would find it." Before Alan could say anything, Lange asked, "What did she write in it?"

Alan opened the cover then looked up to Robin "I do not know, I promised her to never read it, but if she did not want her husband to see it, it must be something important," Robin said. "Thank you Miss Lynch, I will look it over and let you know if it helps. May I give you a ride back to your farm?" Alan asked. "No, I have my horse, he is tied up around the corner," Robin replied. "Please be careful Robin, the sun is almost down," Alan said then tipped his hat to her.

The pair watched as the young woman gave a thin smile then turned to disappear behind the office wall. "How old is she? Seventeen? Eighteen?" Lange asked. "Seventeen I believe," Alan replied while looking at the diary in his hand. "Why would Misses Kiel entrust her diary to such a young girl?" Lange asked. "I do not know, maybe she is the only one she could trust," Alan said puzzled.

"Well Deputy, this is your show so far, I will let you read the book. As for me, I am going to head over to the hotel & get a room," Lange said looking down the street to the only hotel. "I will go out to the cemetery to keep an eye on the grave." Alan said, "I will be back for you in the morning."

Alan grabbed a couple apples from his desk drawer then drove back to the cemetery on the dark country road. He parked his car in front of the gates while looking into the pitch darkness of the cemetery. The diary was sitting on the seat next to Alan, but there was little light to read it.

Alan ate his simple dinner then relaxed as much as he could on the hard seat and tried to sleep. Every time he started to nod off something would make a noise to wake him. Finally he slipped into a deep sleep a little after one in the morning that took him until the sun raised high enough to shine in his eyes. He looked over to the grave of Rebecca Kiel to see nothing was out of place. He then looked to his pocket watch and saw it was only five-thirty. He decided to drive back into town to eat breakfast and shave.

The town was sleepy when Alan drove in. The only businesses open were the grain silo and the corner restaurant next to his office. He walked into the restaurant where a small group of farmers were drinking coffee and talking while their wagons were being unloaded at the silo. Alan sat at the counter and waited for the waitress to walk out of the kitchen. This was a frequent stop for Alan and he did it to see the waitress, Amie, Kenneth Lynch's oldest daughter.

"Morning Alan," Amie said as she exited the kitchen with a pot of coffee. "Good morning Amie," Alan said with a smile, "please give me the usual." Amie pulled a pencil out from behind her ear and replied with a flirtatious tone, "Let's see, three eggs, fried but runny… three strips of bacon and a biscuit with strawberry jam." As she walked back into the kitchen, Alan took note of how she walked.

As he sat patiently waiting for his order, one of the farmers at the table yelled over, "Deputy, I heard you will be digging Rebecca Kiel up this morning." Alan, not knowing what truly to say simply nodded his head in an understating manner. "Deputy," the farmer continued, "I hope you throw the book at George Kiel, he is good for nothing. Never been good! Boy should have been left in the woods when he was born…"

"How's that?" a surprised Alan asked of the old, gruff farmer. "Deputy, you have only lived here five years. You do not know what George was like when he was younger. While his brothers were building farms of their own, he sat around doing nothing. He was constantly in fights in the bars. The man is not worth the price of his boots," the farmer stated while clutching his coffee mug with a firm grip.

"Is there anything else you can tell me about George?" Alan asked as Amie was sliding his plate of food to him. "Hank," another farmer said, "tell the deputy about his first wife." Alan gave a look of surprise, "George had a first wife?" The man took a sip of his coffee and said, "Yes Sir. They were married early, he was seventeen and she was fifteen I believe. Charles set them up in a little house on his farm, but George was mean from the beginning. He drank and stayed out late and of course did not like to work. Well, they were married for about two years I believe it was… Yes, it was the winter and his wife, Melissa was her name, were coming home from the town. Knowing George, he had few drinks in him. Well, they were on the bridge over the creek. Somehow the wagon got too close to the edge and turned over. Melissa went into the water, luckily the wagon missed her, but she was neck deep in freezing water. George got her out, but by the time he got her to the doctor it was too late. She died the next day."

"I never heard this story," Amie said with shock. "Well this is the strangest part deputy," Hank said, "her parents wanted George brought up on charges, said that he purposely murdered their daughter. One of your predecessors said he would investigate, but nothing came to be. That spring her parents decided to move to Galena and retire. Somehow, they never put their farm up for sale, but Charles Kiel now owns the land."

"What year did this happen?" Alan asked of the farmer. "It was the winter of eighteen eighty-nine, I can still remember it to this day as if it just happened," Hank said with a somber tone. Alan took a bite of eggs when he started to think about what the farmer had just said. Alan turned back to the men and asked, "By the way… How do you know we will be exhuming Misses Kiel today?" One of the farmers laughed, "Hell, it's in the newspaper!" Amie grabbed a copy of the paper sitting on the counter and handed it to Alan, "Look here." Alan looked at the headline, 'REBECCA KIEL TO BE EXHUMED TODAY, OFFICALS FEEL SHE

WAS MURDERED'. "This is going to be a circus," Alan said to Amie then took a sip of his coffee.

States Attorney Lange walked into the restaurant and sat down next to Alan. "Deputy," he said, "I hoped you would be here. I need to get some food also, I am just about famished." Alan quickly shoved the paper under his plate, "Did you happen to see the newspaper this morning?" Lange gave him a queer look, "No." Alan just smiled and said to Amie, "Please give Mr. Lange my usual." Amie smiled, "Sure. I will be right back gentlemen."

"I received a message this morning from the front desk. It said that Coroner Knight and Doctor Richards will be here on the seven o'clock train," Lange said. "We can stop by the Kiel's farm and tell them to come along to the cemetery," Alan said, "the sexton and his sons live not far from the cemetery. I am sure they will be happy to help."

Amie placed the plate of food in front of Lange. "My, my, this looks good, but deputy, how can you live on such little food?" Lange asked with a snicker. "Well that is a good amount for me, besides, I eat slowly so I can enjoy the company," Alan said as he winked at Amie. As Lange was eating, the group of farmers got up and paid their bills. Hank turned to Alan and said, "Remember deputy, that Kiel is no good. I hope you get him." As the farmers walked out, Lange looks to Alan and asked, "What was that all about?" Alan wiped his mouth clean with a white cloth then said,

"Sometimes the men in this town gossip more than the women."

As Lange was eating his breakfast, Alan did his best to talk with Amie. "Your sister came to see me last night. She had Rebecca Kiel's diary," Alan said. "She told me she was here but swore me to not speak a word of it with anyone," Amie said as she wiped the counter down with a damp cloth. "Did you speak with the Kiel's much?" Alan asked. "No… I really did not. Rebecca would wave to me when she saw me but other than that, we did not communicate. George is odd. I did not like the way he would look at me," Amie said with a soft tone to Alan.

"I hate to break this up, but the train should be here soon. We better go over there to meet the men," Lange said as he pushed the empty plate to Amie. "Put our meals on my tab," Alan said with a wink to Amie, "I will see you for lunch I am sure." Amie smiled, "I will be here."

Lange and Alan walked out of the restaurant into the early morning dampness. "The street car should be here in a few minutes. Oh, have you had a chance to look at the diary yet?" Lange asked. "No, I hope to this afternoon after our days' work," Alan said, "maybe it will shine a light on what happened to Rebecca." Lange looked down at his watch, "I hope digging her up will do that."

The street car stopped with a screech at the platform right on time. As the coroner and Doctor

Richards walked off carrying three black bags they looked to see Alan and Lange walking up to meet them. "Coroner, Doctor…," Alan said, "I hope your ride down was good." The doctor retorted bluntly while rubbing his lower back, "They still need to fix that damn track!" As Alan was about to tell them where the car was, a group of four men came off of the street car, each of them wearing suits, cleaned and pressed precisely. One carried a brief case and each looked very out of place for Mill Grove.

"I'll be damned…," Lange whispered. "That is Charles Kiel's attorneys, the best he could get from Chicago," coroner Knight said. As the street car pulled away, it reveled Charles sitting in the driver's seat of his automobile. When he saw the men, he motioned to them. They approached the automobile and got in filling the seats to beyond capacity.

Charles drove over toward Lange and asked, "Shall we head out to the grave yard?" Lange looked into the car to see the lawyers crammed inside, "Yes, but please remember to bring George out with you. He must be present." Charles clenched his teeth and said dryly with little expression, "Oh, he will be there." Alan waited for the litter of lawyers to leave before he said, "Let's get into my car and get out there. We can stop by the sexton's house and ask for his assistance."

Chapter 4

Alan and the officials from Glasford drove to the sexton's house just down the road from the Mount Elm Cemetery. Alan stepped out of the automobile and approached the dilapidated house, its porch roof rotting to the point where it was starting to fall in. A tall, wiry man wearing bib overalls walked onto the porch smoking a pipe.

"Deputy," he said with a gurgled voice. "Mister Franks, I need your...," Alan started to say but was abruptly interrupted. "I know what you are here for deputy, I read today's newspaper. My sons and me will be right there. But I must confess, this is not a very Christian thing to do," the man stated with a deep southern accent. "Neither is murder," Alan stated, "we will see you there."

Alan jumped back into the automobile and drove the short drive to the cemetery. Charles and his lawyers were waiting along with George who was sitting on the back of a wooden wagon. The horses harnessed to the wagon were enjoying the grass along the road totally unaware of what was transpiring. Mister Franks and his sons came closely behind Alan in their wagon. With them were three shovels and a pry bar, the only tools they would need.

Mister Franks stepped past the men to unlock the gate. He pushed it open with a grunt, the gate creaking as it opened slowly. His sons grabbed their tools and walked to Rebecca's grave. With the large oak trees providing shade for the three men, they worked rapidly only taking a half of an hour until they reached the top of the coffin. The earth smelled fresh as they worked the dirt. "Do you gentlemen want to examine her down here or up there?" Mister Franks asked looking out of the hole. "Up here please," the coroner said. The men lifted the coffin and slid it up onto the ground at the feet of the coroner.

Franks grabbed the pry bar and was about to start removing the nails until Lange stopped him. "Wait one minute sir, I must read this aloud before we begin," Lange said as he pulled a piece of paper out of his suit jacket, "On this the nineteenth day of July, nineteen hundred and twelve. I, States Attorney Robert Lange, have been charged with the duty of exhuming the body of Rebecca Kiel and observing the autopsy of said Kiel by Coroner Knight. This duty was given to me by the Honorable William Hollingshead of the first district court in the city of Glasford, state of Illinois."

Charles crossly grabbed the pry bar from the sexton's hand and said, "Can we just get on with this already?!" Lange took the pry bar from Charles and gave it back to Mister Franks, "Go ahead…"

Franks carefully pried the coffin cover loose. Everyone present but George stood around the casket as the cover was removed. He kept his seat on the back of his wagon, his head held low along with his mood. When he would raise his head, he would look out to the road and the cornfields beyond. He never looked to the cemetery; he never looked at the corpse of his wife lying in the pine box.

Rebecca looked to be placed with care in the coffin. She still worn the dress she had on the day of the murder, the only item missing was her apron. The bullet hole in her temple was quite visible; her skin pale, her eyes open. As Charles' attorneys observed, coroner Knight knelt down and turned Rebecca's head to reveal a hole behind her left ear. He reached over to one of the bags and removed a small metal ruler. He held it to the hole behind her ear and then he turned her head to measure the hole on her temple. "It is the same size," Knight stated. Doctor Richards noted this on his note pad as ashes from his cigarette fell onto the paper.

Coroner Knight next reached into his bag and removed a small case. He unbuttoned it and opened it to reveal surgical tools that shined in the hot sun. "Gentlemen, if any of you have a weak stomach, I ask that you remove yourself to another part of the cemetery," Knight stated as he looked up at the observers. Alan could feel his stomach tighten, but did not want to be the first to walk away. To his amazement, no one moved an inch.

Knight removed a long pair of tweezers from his case. He carefully placed it into the hole on Rebecca's temple. He slowly inserted the tweezers trying to feel the resistance of the bullet. "I think I feel it," Knight said. He allowed the tweezers to open and carefully grabbed hold of the bullet. He slowly, carefully pulled the tweezers out of her head. Once in the sunlight, he looked carefully at the bloody bullet.

"Doctor, please give me one of the jars from your bag," the coroner said. The doctor removed a small mason jar with a shiny steel lead. The coroner placed the bullet into the jar and tightened the lid. "Please mark this as temple and place in your notes it was at a depth of two inches," he said to doctor Richards who was rolling another cigarette.

Coroner Knight now turned his attention to the second hole. Again he carefully inserted the tweezers into the hole. This time the tweezers went in deeper. "I do not feel the bullet yet," Knight stated, "Doctor please note that this hole is at a different angel from that of the temple." He continued to feel around then quickly released the tension of the tweezers. Gently he pulled the tweezers out; on the tip was another bullet.

"Deputy, please place George Kiel under arrest," Lange barked. "This does not mean my son had anything to do with this!" Charles cried as one of the attorneys motioned at him to remain quiet.

Alan walked down to George to do as he was told and place George under arrest.

"George, please give me your hands," Alan said as he removed a pair of handcuffs from his belt and placed them onto George's hands. "George Kiel, I am placing you under arrest for the murder of your wife, Rebecca and your mother-in-law Martha Vogal," Alan stated as he could feel anger starting to grow but remained calm and professional.

"Coroner, are you finished?" Mister Franks asked. "No," Lange stated, "Coroner I would like a sample of both the tissue around the wounds and of the skull where the bullets entered." Alan could feel his stomach tighten again. "Do you really need the wounds? I should have the tools I need…," coroner Knight said. Lange looked down to the corpse, "Yes. I believe the jury will need to see what that man did."

Coroner Knight took a scalpel and carefully cut about one inch around the wounds to remove the skin. Each wound sample was placed in their own jars. Doctor Richards added formaldehyde to the jars to preserve the tissue and then sealed the jars tight. Next the coroner used a small drill to make holes so as to use a hand saw to cut the bones of the skull.

At this moment Alan took George to his car. He knew he could not see any more, it was both grotesque and hard to witness because he would see

Rebecca when she came to town. He placed George in the automobile and stood next to the road watching the wind swirl up dust. Alan thought when he left Chicago he would not have to deal with crimes like this ever again. George sat in the back quiet, motionless, almost as if this was just a bad dream and waiting to awake in his bed.

Alan looked back to see George sitting there in a world of his own. He wanted to take George and shake him, beat him, ask him why he did this. Why he would hurt such a sweet woman. But Alan knew he needed to keep calm and allow the law he swore to uphold to take care of George Kiel.

"Deputy," Lange yelled from the gravesite, "please come here." Alan approached the men but made sure to not look at the body. "Deputy, I will take custody of George and escort him back to Glasford for a bail hearing in the morning," Lange stated. Coroner Knight packed the evidence into the third bag he brought with him. He tied the handle with a golden twine to make sure it would not be tampered with until the evidence was safely back in his office.

Charles and his attorneys stood off to the side and discussed what would be their next move. "Sexton… you can seal the casket and place it back in the ground," Lange said, "Mister Kiel, I will let you know what time the bail hearing will be tomorrow as soon as I know." Charles did his best to remain calm, "Thank you, I will be there. I will make sure my son is dismissed of these charges." Charles walked to his automobile with his attorneys followed like ducklings chasing a mother duck.

"Come on, I will get you back for the twelve o'clock streetcar," Alan said to the men. They left the grave yard as Mister Franks sealed the casket. The sun was high and the winds were picking up moving the trees about the men as they worked. George sat between Knight and Richards on the way back to town. He never said a word, he never made an expression.

Alan parked his automobile next to the platform. The town was more active at this time. As people walked by the car and saw George inside, the gossip started running like wildfire. It was only a matter of minutes before most of the town knew of George's fate. As the streetcar rumbled to a stop in front of the platform, the men got out of the car and waited for the motormen to open the door. Lange took hold of George's left arm and escorted him onto the car.

"Deputy, I will let you know about the bail hearing," Lange said. "Please do. Maybe I will know before the newspaper does," Alan said with a chuckle. Lange went onto the streetcar and squeezed George toward the window. George looked out at Alan and the small group of townspeople that collected to see what is happening. As George stared at the people, he did not make an expression, his face was stone. He then turned his head forward and waited for the streetcar to start moving.

Alan went back to his office after the men departed for Glasford. The quiet was comforting over the dealings of the past few days. He had just sat down when there was a knock at the door. "Come in," Alan said hoping to have been left alone for the afternoon. The door opened to reveal Amie holding a plate with a plaid towel on top. "Alan, I hoped you may be hungry for some of my fried chicken," Amie said with a smile. Alan, with his stomach still rolling from the autopsy, smiled politely and said "Thank you Amie, I am always ready for your chicken."

Amie placed the plate in front of him and removed the towel. Four pieces of fried chicken, two biscuits and a pile of mashed potatoes covered in milk gravy all stared back at him. Next to the food were two sets of forks and knives. "I thought maybe you could share your lunch with me," Amie said with a flirtatious tone. "I would love that," Alan said with a smile.

Amie pulled one the chairs up to the desk and sat next to Alan. "Who is running the restaurant?" Alan asked. "Robin is helping out. I told her I needed a break," Amie said. Alan, swallowed the first delicious bite of the chicken and asked, "Can I ask you a few questions about Robin?" Amie, with a surprised look on her face said, "I come here and you want to talk about Robin?" Alan looked up at Amie with a smile and said, "We can talk about you in a few minutes… This is the diary I told you about this morning." Alan pulled Rebecca's diary out of the desk drawer and placed it in front of Amie.

"Well, what is in it?" Amie asked with great curiosity. "I do not know, I have not read it yet. Did you know that Robin talked with Rebecca?" Alan asked then took a bite of mashed potatoes. "No and I am sure father did not also. While he would help if George asked for anything, father did not like him. Mother does not like him either. We were always told to stay away from the Kiel's," Amie said.

"Did you father ever say why he did not like him?" Alan asked. "Well, no, but after what we heard this morning, I have a good guess. My father did say something queer last night to mother. He said that he heard that Misses Vogal had papers drawn up to lease her farm to James Palmer last week," Amie said as she cut up one of the pieces of chicken.

"James Palmer… is he related to August?" Alan asked. "Yes, he is Augusts' older brother. He owns a large farm over in Hazelton," Amie said. "Well if that is the case, where would that leave George & Rebecca?" Alan asked softly as if thinking out loud. "I do not know. I am guessing that August would take the farm over and George would be out of a job. Of course my father said he is not much of a farmer," Amie said with a slight giggle. "You know, I have heard that a lot over the past few days…," Alan said

"So enough about Robin and Rebecca and murder… let's talk about us," Amie said with a hint of innocence in her voice. Alan raised his right eyebrow while he wiped the grease from his mouth with the towel. Alan liked Amie a lot, but was afraid that her father would never approve of him. He was from the city; he did not know how to grow a houseplant let alone a whole farm. He was not even good with his hands.

"So, what would you like to talk about?" Alan asked with slight curiosity. "Well, there is a dance tomorrow night at the town hall. I still have not heard anyone ask me if I wanted to go…," Amie said looking off to the side with her blue eyes. Alan chuckled, "Well, there is August Palmer; he might want to go with you…" Amie looked back to Alan with her eyes large, "That is not who I am talking about!"

Alan started to giggle, "I guess I could take you….. That is if you would like." Amie said with great excitement, "Wow, what an offer!" Alan straightened up in his chair and with a serious tone asked, "Miss Lynch, would you please allow me to escort you to the dance tomorrow night?" Amie smiled, "Why yes Mister Johnson I would love to. Well I better get back to the restaurant; Robin may have sold it to Gypsies by now."

Before Amie stood fully up from her chair, she stole a kiss from Alan's lips. "Is that a preview of tomorrow night?" Alan asked surprised. "Maybe," Amie stated with a smile. She picked up the empty plate and placed the towel back on it. Alan watches closely as she walked to the door. "What time should I pick you up tomorrow?" Alan asked before she could open the door. Amie turned and said, "Six sounds good and Alan, you really do need to come in and talk with my father for at least a few minutes…"

Alan gave a slight grin, "Oh I will." Amie opened the door, turned once more toward Alan and seemingly kissed the air. Alan smiled, "I cannot wait until tomorrow night!" Amie shook her head in disbelief with a large smile then walked out the door

The silence of his office was almost deafening. He thought for a moment about Amie which lead him to think about August and the love he held for Rebecca. The recent events have taught Alan that we do not control our fates as much as we think we do.

Alan picked up the diary and was just opening the cover when the phone rang. "Deputy Johnson," Alan said. "This is Lange; the bail hearing is set for eight tomorrow morning. Will you be coming?" Alan heard the statement that came through the static filled line, but was not ready to deal with it. "No, I have a lot to do here, please let me know how it comes out," Alan said. "I will…

have you had a chance to read that diary yet?" Lange asked with urgency. "No, I will start it right away," Alan replied. "Well get to it, I am trying to build a case here. Hopefully that diary may have some needed information," Lange barked.

Alan started to feel like he has been put in his place a bit. "Oh by the way," Lange continued, "I saw the paper. That paper seems to know things before we do. I wonder how they get their information." There was larger burst of static and then a click on the phone like a circuit disconnected. "Johnson, you still there?" Lange asked. "Yes, I am here," Alan said. "Must be a branch on a wire," Lange said. "Oh yes a branch… I just wonder how the paper finds its information out…," Alan said with a touch of humor. "Yes, we need to find out…," Lange said with anger, "Well I will call you after the bail hearing… good bye."

Before Alan could reply the line clicked off and Lange was gone. "I should have just stayed in Chicago…," Alan said out loud to the empty room.

Chapter 5

Alan made himself comfortable in his wooden chair and while sitting in the stream of the brass desk fan, he opened Rebecca's diary. Alan read the book aloud as if someone was in the room listening to him retell the woman's life in personal details.

June 10, 1902 - Tomorrow George and I will be married. I love him with all of my heart, but I fear that he will never be a tame man. I fear his drinking, but mother said all men drink and I should learn to live with it like she did with fathers'. Mother told me this morning that she would like for George to run her farm. I do not know if George would want to do that. He despises his father and his farm. I do not know what George would like to do. I never told anyone, but while I love George, I do not feel comfortable with his age. Mother introduced us and it seems she forced us together after that point.

The next page jumped all of the way to nineteen-seven. Many pages in-between seemed to be missing from the book. Did they contain anything important? As he started to read the remaining pages, Alan hoped of finding needed clues, but nothing was found. Most of it appeared to talk about trivial things like how beautiful the day was or how the flowers smelled that day. He turned through the pages, but it was more of the same.

December 24, 1909 - We were at father's house for Christmas Eve dinner. George's brothers and their families were there. His brother Michael asked George when we would be having a family. I could see the pain on Georges face. He joked that we would someday. I wish he could tell his family the truth, well at least his father and brothers. I know it is not Georges fault. I guess he does not find me attractive anymore, but I remember he had this problem since we were married. I do not know what to do. I would like a family of my own, but I guess it will never happen. Sometimes he comes to bed and I touch him, but he coils back. I wish I could be the woman he wanted. I do not understand men and their ways.

Alan, now more confused than ever, did not know if this was a true clue. Did this prove that George did not really love his wife? Did he love her, but could not find a way to show it? The biggest question Alan had in his mind is what was on the missing pages? It appears they were torn in anger. Did George find her diary? More importantly, did the pages hold information he did not want anyone to find? This book seems to raise more questions than provide answers. Further in, more pages seem to be missing.

June 4, 1910 - August came to me today while George was in the barn. I believe he was fresh with me, but I am unsure what to do. A good wife would know what to do; she knows the love of her husband and would not even consider the advances of another man. But I felt good at what he did. It felt right, but I know it was not. I do not know what to do, I have no one to talk with about this. I have never felt so alone.

June 5, 1910 - I told mother about August. She wanted to let him go, but I protested. I told her that I felt good about how he treated me. She does not understand. She does know the problems I have with George. She does not understand that I want to be loved. I want to be held. I just wish I could have told August.

Alan sat in amazement. According to August, he did not make that hard of advances, but to Rebecca's words, it seems more than that. The question Alan had in his mind was if George knew about this? Did this cause him to kill her? So many questions, but so few answers.

Alan continued to read. Page after page, but nothing of interest. Back to the same, how the flowers looked, how pretty the sky was. Nothing of August, nothing of George. Maybe this was a clue in itself. Maybe Rebecca could not handle the pains in her life. Perhaps the flowers and sky made her feel better. Alan sat and looked out the window. The sky was growing darker with another summer storm approaching. He turned on his desk lamp to be able to read better.

January 17, 1912 - Mother and I went to town to pick up fabric and baking supplies. We went past one of the taverns on the edge of town. I would not expect such a place of filth to be in our town and to be open so early. As we walked past I saw a man enter, it was George. He promised me that he would quit drinking. I destroyed all of the bottles of alcohol in the house, but I cannot destroy the tavern. I confronted George about his drinking after dinner. He pushed me to the floor and said he would not be told by any woman how to lead his life. I do not believe I can handle this anymore. I love August. I do not love George. I must find a way out.

February 10, 1912 - I have not written in a long time. I did not feel like it. It seems I have lost my way in life. I do not know if I will ever find happiness. I am angry that I was allowed to be coerced into this marriage. I knew mother needed a man to run the farm, but George was not the man she thought or hoped he was. That is why we hired August. Now I wished we did not hire him either. I cannot tell him the love I have for him. I cannot live the life I want. George is not home much anymore. I do not know where he is. Sometimes I see him coming out of the barn. I think he must have whiskey hidden out there, but I want to stay away. August lives in the barn and I cannot be near him. I love him so very much. At least I think I love him.

Alan placed the book down on his desk. He rubbed his eyes as they were tired from the book and the day's events. The wind was blowing dust clouds off of the streets and thunder rumbled in the distance. Alan looked up to the wall clock, four thirty-four. The afternoon flew by, but he still has more questions than answers. He picked the book up and after letting out a thunderous yawn, continued to read.

March 29, 1912 - I thought George would kill me tonight. He took his revolver and placed it to my head. He came home drunk. He was so drunk he came into mother's room thinking it was ours. She yelled for him to leave, he stumbled out and went to the bookcase. He pulled many books off the shelf and threw them to the floor. He had a gun hidden behind them; I never knew he had a gun. He went back to my mother's room and aimed at her. I grabbed the gun. He hit me knocking me to the floor then grabbed me by the hair, pulled me up and placed the gun to my temple. I could hear the hammer pulling back, I cried for him to stop. I begged for my life as I cried. He let my hair go causing me to fall to the floor. He left the house leaving the gun on the floor. I do not know where he went and I hope he does not return. I told mother I want him gone. I want to divorce him. Mother said no, she said we need him or we will lose the farm. I told her August could handle the farm and I told her that I love him. She slapped me telling me I not her daughter. Her daughter would not cheat on her husband. I told her I did not cheat but I love August. I wanted to be with him. I am so sad. I feel like I am dying inside. I do not know why this is happening to me. All I want is the love of a good man.

Alan now was finding the answers he needed. He was also angered by what he read and wished Rebecca would just come to him for help. Surely he could have saved her from George.

March 30, 1912 - George did not return until this afternoon. He was his usual self; quiet and tense, hiding in the barn with the animals. This morning I took his gun to August and asked him to hide it. He asked why. I did not want to tell him what happened. I kept my hair down to hide the bruise on my face. I just told him that George was drinking more and I feared he might hurt himself. August honored my wishes. I hugged him and thanked him. I wanted to keep holding him, but I could not. I could not love him like I want.

Alan jumped and dumped the diary to the floor when a large crash of thunder rocked his office. He looked out to see the dusty street now filling with water and mud. He reached down to pick up the book and saw a shadow outside his window during a flash of lightning. He swiftly got to his feet and went to the window. No one was there. Next he went to the door and opened it, but again no one was to be found. It must have just been his imagination. Alan sat back down in his chair and opened the diary to where he left off.

April 6, 1912 - Mother said she had contacted a lawyer in Glasford and also James Palmer. She wants to lease the farm to James for him and August to run. She also said she will ask if I can divorce

George. She said she is sorry and that it is her fault for the life I have. I told her that it is my fault because I wanted to marry George. I did love him in the beginning, but now I just want to be free. I asked where we would live. She and James agreed that he did not need the house so we can stay. He would farm the land and she would earn rent.

April 18, 1912 - George found my diary tonight. He started to rip pages out of it, but I grabbed it from him before he learned about mother's plans, before he learned of my love for August. I picked up the torn pages and hid them in the wood box next to the fireplace. I went outside for air and to escape him. While I was outside, I saw Robin Lynch walking on the road, throwing sticks to her dog. I asked her if she could hide my diary for me. I knew she is old enough to entrust her to my diary, but I told her not to read it. She promised she would not and to ask her whenever I wanted it. I pray I can trust her. I do not think I can trust anyone. I feel so alone. As I write this we are sitting under the apple tree that looks over the kitchen porch. I see in Robin myself in my younger years. I wish I would have had the knowledge of life I have now. She and her sister are such beautiful young women. Many times I wish I would have been more attractive. Maybe my life would have been different.

May 20, 1912 - I asked Robin for my diary today. Not much has changed, but the lawyer told mother I could file for divorce, but the chances of a judge approving it are very slim. It appears I am more property than a wife. August said that his brother will take the lease as soon as the harvest is over. I do not know what George will do, but I am not worried. Anything must be better than this.

Alan stood up to stretch. The storm was almost finished outside and people were returning to the now muddied streets. Alan noticed a growing rainbow out the window as the hot sun returned from the parting clouds. He walked to the window to get a better glance, but he found something of more interest; Charles Kiel walking into the general store alone. Alan stood at the door watching for Charles to return and wondering if he was the shadow in the window. After about five minutes he felt it would be better to continue to read the diary but suddenly Charles emerged from the general store. He had two cans of lamp oil and a brown package then went swiftly to his car to leave.

Being the curious type, Alan walked across the street splashing water as he walk into the general store. The shop owner, Karl Green, was a pleasant fellow, always wanting to help. "Hello Alan," Karl said with a pleasant tone. "Karl, can you tell me what Charles Kiel just bought?" Alan asked. "Well… a few cans of lamp oil and one pound worth of oil rags." Karl responded with a puzzled tone. "Oil rags?" Alan asked. "Yes, you know, cloth rags to clean up oil and grease," Karl said. "Did he buy anything else? Alan asked. "um, no, nothing else… do you think he is up to no good?" Karl asked with a surprised look. "I do not know, but I am going to find out," Alan stated with content.

Alan ran to the door and across the street to his car. He started it then jumped in. He drove as fast as he could toward the Kiel farm. The road was slick from the storm and he was having a hard time keeping the car on the road. He could see Charles ahead of him about one half of a mile. Charles drove past his house and kept going. "He is going to Rebecca's house!" Alan said out loud.

Alan had the pedal to the floor but the car kept sliding on the road. He had to slow down to keep control. He could see Charles' car turn off the road to the right. Alan kept pace and arrived in about one minute to find Charles' car abandoned in the driveway. Alan looked around but did not see Charles so he ran to the house. "Charles Kiel, are you in here?" Alan yelled into the house, his hand on his revolver. He heard footsteps to his right; he turned and saw August Palmer "What is wrong Deputy?" August asked. "Did you see Charles go into the house?" Alan asked winded. "No... I was in the barn. I did not see where he went," August replied.

"Charles Kiel, are you in this house?" Alan asked again just as he heard the floor creak inside. Charles appeared in the doorway. "What do you want Deputy?" Charles demanded. "Charles Kiel step out of the house slowly and walk to the end of porch," Alan said pulling his revolver. Charles did as he was told.

"What are you doing here?" Alan asked. "I was checking on the house for George," Charles barked back. "You do not have a right to be on this property Kiel," Alan yelled with authority. "I have every right boy. This is my son's house!" Charles yelled back. August stayed to the side of Alan looking as if a war was about to begin before his eyes.

"This is the property of the estate of Martha Vogel. This is also the crime scene in an ongoing murder case. You are trespassing Mister Kiel," Alan said quickly losing his temper. "I was not told I could not enter this house. You never said one thing about this house, Johnson," Charles said. "I am telling you now. You were seen buying lamp oil and oil rags at the general store. What did you do with them?" Alan asked.

"They are in my car. Am I not allowed to buy those items Deputy?" Charles asked as he swatted at mosquitos that were on the attack. "What do you have planned for the items?" Alan asked as he placed his gun back into its holster. "I plan to use the oil in my lamps and the rags to clean up around the barn," Charles said with innocence. Alan shook his head in disagreement, "You have electricity Mister Kiel…" Charles started to lose his temper again, "It went out during the storm! It could be out for days before I get a repairman here!"

"Do you want to know what I think you will use the items for Mister Kiel?" Alan asked. "Please, enlighten me Deputy…," Charles stated with fervor. "I believe you were about to commit the act of arson. Now, please leave this property before you are sharing a cell with your son for the crime of trespassing and attempted arson," Alan stated. Charles stepped off of the porch and walked toward Alan, "Now why would I burn this fine house?" Alan stood stared the man down, "I don't know… but I am sure going to find out."

Charles walked past Alan and toward his car. "Deputy," he said as he walked away, "you do know I have many powerful friends and I can make your job disappear in a heartbeat." Alan retorted with a straight face, "Yes you can Mister Kiel… but that would not look good to the jury that will hold yours sons' fate."

Charles cranked his car to start it. "Son of a bitch," Charles yelled as it would not start, "August? Where the hell are you?" August was leaning against the wall of the house, "I'm right here Mister Kiel… please… let me help." August walked over reluctantly and cranked the engine over. It started with the first try and Charles threw it into gear before August could fully get clear. August jumped to the side just in time to be missed by the left headlamp as the car turned swiftly. Alan just shook his head in disbelief.

"Did you see that Deputy? That man is crazy!" August exclaimed with anger. "I saw it and I think there is something desperately wrong with that man," Alan said. "Do you really think he was going to burn the house?" August asked. "I would not put nothing past him," Alan replied, "August, please keep an eye on the house. I will be back in the morning to search it." August shook his head in agreement, "Sure… what are you looking for?" Alan shrugged his shoulders, "When I know I will tell you. See you in the morning."

Alan returned to town by way of Charles Kiel's farm. As he passed, he slowed to see the house was lit up with the light of electricity, not oil lamps. Alan went back to his office to finish the diary. He sat at his desk to see the diary stared back at him like the missing piece of a puzzle, but Alan did not feel it would be the simple. One page was left to be read. It appeared that Rebecca did not feel like writing anymore in her diary, but she made the effort to do it on last time.

July 16, 1912 - August was not at dinner tonight, mother asked that he eat in his room, she needed to talk with George alone. Mother told George of the lease at dinner this evening. She explained that James and August would be far better farmers for this land than he could be. George sat still in his chair. I was so afraid he would do something to us, but he actually looked relived. Mother further added that we would be keeping the house, but that George should take a job to help provide for me.

He sat in his chair motionless and quiet. We ate dinner quietly; in peace. When George was finished he left the house and hitched up his wagon. He left for town; left for the tavern I am sure. I wish I could have told him I wanted a divorce. It is almost midnight and he has not returned. I pray he is safe.

Chapter 6

Alan tried to sleep that night, but he was haunted with the fact that he could have helped Rebecca if she had only told him. He was angered by the smugness of Charles Kiel and the fact that his money can free George. He dreamed of his love for Amie and he dreaded the thought of talking with her father.

Saturday morning, the day of the dance, came quickly. The first thought Alan had was not the dance or even Amie, but what Charles Kiel was trying to find or destroy in the house. He shaved and dressed quickly, then went to the kitchen in his small framed house to make breakfast. Alan did not know how to cook well but he could make coffee with his electric hot plate. The hot plate that would shock him on at least a few occasions a week. Alan made the coffee then placed the pot on the hot plate. Alan carefully touched the knob and turned it to the right. "No shock today," Alan said to himself. After a few minutes the strong smell of coffee told Alan that his breakfast was ready. He turned the knob off. "Damn!" Alan yelled as he was shocked, "I do not know if electricity will ever be useful."

He quickly drank a few cups of coffee and then was out the door with haste. The coffee was breakfast for him, unless he wanted to see Amie, then he would eat a large breakfast at the restaurant. Alan did want to see Amie, but knew he could not let his emotions for her color the job he needed to do this morning.

The day was hot, very hot like the whole summer has been. The early morning July sun was quickly burning the haze and fog off of the fields and drying out the roads that were still wet from the night before. Alan drove past Charles' house where all seemed normal as his help were turning out the cows to the pasture. His car was absent, but Alan knew that he must be on his was to Glasford for George's bail hearing.

Alan pulled into the gravel driveway of the Vogal homestead to see August out in the field thrashing the wheat. He waved to Alan, who waved right back. Alan entered the house through the kitchen door where he saw that blood still stained the floor and Marta's chair was still overturned. The dough on the table was solid and cracked; the apples had rotted to mush and flies were buzzing around them. Alan **held** his handkerchief over his mouth and nose as the smell was becoming overwhelming. He quickly moved to open the windows of the kitchen and then the windows of the parlor. Next to the outside door in the parlor was a hat rack holding two worn work hats and one proper homburg hat. "These must be George's," Alan said to himself.

Alan quickly found the wood box near the fireplace. He opened the lid to reveal five pieces of split oak. At first glance, nothing was seen but the wood. He felt around, but nothing was felt but

73

wood and shards of dried bark. Alan removed the wood from the box and looked inside. Nothing; it was empty. Did George find with papers? Did that cause him to finally kill Rebecca?

The house was not lush, not rich, but well loved. Rebecca kept the house clean, items in their place. The parlor held a small couch and two cushioned chairs. A rocking chair set next to the fireplace. It was well worn and looked to be handmade, perhaps this was Mister Vogal's chair, Alan thought. Little else was in the room except for a small table with an oil lamp and a clock on the mantle of the fireplace.

Alan moved to the formal dining room. A polished table sat bare with four polished chairs surrounding it as a glass fronted cabinet held chinaware in the far corner. There were two drawers under the cabinet. Alan opened one to find polished silverware. He closed the drawer and opened the other to find papers. Alan removed them and looked for anything of importance. Most of the papers were paid receipts from the stores in town. Nothing looked odd or of importance.

Alan walked to the staircase. It was plain with worn, painted wooden steps. As he went upstairs the boards creaked under his feet. At the top of the stairs was a small room that appeared to be used as an office. A roll topped desk sat next to the only window, against the opposite wall was a bookcase. "This must be where the gun was," Alan said out loud as he noticed the books were not placed with the care Alan thought Rebecca would use. He opened the top of the desk causing an avalanche of papers to fall onto the floor. Alan bent to pick them up; many were yellow from age and the print was disappearing. One piece of paper was a reccipt from eighteen seventy-eight for seed. Nothing looked new; the desk must have not been used in years.

Alan turned his attention to the bookcase. The books on the upper shelf were haphazardly placed, the lower shelves were immaculate. Possibly George looked for his gun before the murder Alan thought. He moved the books on the top shelf around, nothing was behind them. Alan bent over and looked at the lower shelves. He moved books around, but nothing was there.

Alan walked out to the hallway. The next door on the same side of the hallway was closed. He opened the door with a solid push as it was stiff and swelled with humidity. The room held one bed with a quilt on top. This must have been Marta's room Alan thought. The room was more decorated then the rest of the house. The walls were covered in a bright wallpaper as wilted flowers sat in a vase on a small table. Next to the table was a rocking chair holding a ball of yarn and needles. In the opposite side corner of the room was an armoire. Alan opened it to find women's clothing. On the single shelf near the top of the cabinet, was a jewelry box.

Alan reached for the box and opened it to reveal the torn pages from a book. With one glance he knew they were from Rebecca's diary. Alan placed the papers in his pocket for later reading. There was nothing below the papers, not even jewelry. Alan reached to feel around on the shelf only to feel more papers. He pulled them out and saw they were the leasing agreement for the farm. The signatures of both Marta and James Palmer were on it. It was dated July twelfth. Marta must have had to work up the courage to tell George.

With the leasing agreement firmly in his hand, Alan proceeded to the room across the hall. This was the bedroom for Rebecca and George. The room was like the rest; clean but plain. The furniture was worn; showing its age and the blankets appeared to be mended many times with care. On the window wall there was a small dressing table with a wooden stool. Alan imagined Rebecca sitting in front of the mirror brushing her hair. Nothing looked like it held clues to the murders. Alan walked out of the room without disturbing a thing.

Alan was happy to find the missing papers from the diary but was unhappy to not find the clue that would secure Georges conviction. He walked downstairs and exited the house to find August sitting near the windmill slowly dumping water over his head to keep cool. August got up and walked to Alan. "Did you find anything Deputy?" August inquired. "A few things, but nothing that I would warrant burning the house down like I think Charles was going to do last night," Alan replied.

"I slept in the opening of the loft door last night to keep watch on the house and also stay cool," August said. "All was quiet?" Alan asked. "Yes, I did not hear or see a thing," August said, "I am sure I would have heard anyone coming around."

Alan worked up the courage to open an old wound that appears to have cut August deeply. "August, we talked about your relationship with Rebecca the other day. You said you did not show your feeling to her, correct?" Alan asked. August swept his wet hair back then said, "Yes, that is true. I cannot tell you how much I wanted to..." Alan took his hat off to fan himself, "Did George have any clue of your feelings?" August looked away, "No… well, I may have out of anger…"

"How do you mean August?" Alan asked with curiosity. "Two or three months ago, George stumbled into the barn. He was drunk, stupid and came looking for a fight. I was more than happy to oblige, but he did not have a fight in. He was so drunk he took one swing and landed on the stall floor. His face full of manure was a good look for him," August said then laughed.

Alan pressed August a little further, "When did you tell him about your feelings?" August looked down and kicked at the dirt with his boots, "He laid on the floor laughing and said he did not want to fight me, he wanted to kill that bitch he married." August's face grew red and his voice trembled as he continued, "When he said that I lost all control and kicked him in the gut as hard as I could. I then placed my boot on his throat and told him that if he ever hurt her I would kill him. I told him that I loved Rebecca and that I would be a far better husband than him."

"What did he do after this?" Alan asked. "I took my boot off of his throat and acted like I was going to kick him. He curled up in defense and started to cry. I told him to go sleep it off. He got up and stumbled out to the corn crib where he passed out on the ground. I left his sorry ass there," August said with disgust.

"Why did you not tell me this before?" Alan asked. "I was afraid you would arrest me or thought I was the one that killed Rebecca," August said in a somber tone. "If I could give you a reward for kicking that S-O-B I would have, but I do need to know everything. Is there anything else that you need to tell me?" Alan asked with an official tone.

"The day Rebecca asked me to hide the gun. She hugged me. God, I wanted to hold on, I never wanted to let her go but she pulled away. I told her I would do anything for her. She said in a soft voice that soon she would be able to hug me longer. Then she walked away, I do not know what she meant by that," August said trying to hold back tears. "I have a feeling what she wanted to tell you that she was going to try to divorce George," Alan said.

"She was going to divorce George? I did not know…," August said quietly. "Well as far as I can tell, he did not either," Alan said. August took his hat off his head, wiped the sweat from his forehead with his right hand and said in a shaky voice, "Why did that bastard do this!? Why could I have not saved her from him?" Alan placed his left hand on August's shoulder and said, "August I do not know why she did not tell you…" Alan stopped himself, he did not want to tell August about the love Rebecca held for him.

"I really have to get back to work deputy… I have to work… to forget this," August said placing his hat back on his head. "Okay August, but I do need to tell Lange what you said. He may have to call you into court," Alan stated. "I will be happy to go into court and look that son of bitch right in the face as I tell the judge what he said and has done the whole time I have worked here," August said with anger back in his voice. August started to walk back to the field but was stopped by Alan. "August," Alan said, "You are sure you never told Rebecca about your gun?" August turned, "I am positive deputy. As God as my witness I wish I would have used it on George."

Alan went back to his office to call Lange and tell him about what he had found in the diary.

"Sarah, get me States Attorney Lange please," Alan said. "Deputy, he has been trying to reach you all morning. The last time he called he asked me to tell you that there is no bail," Sarah said. "Did he say anything else?" Alan asked, "Yes, he would like for you to call him Monday morning with a report of the book you were to read…," Sarah replied with curiosity in her voice.

"Say Deputy," Sarah continued, "are you taking anyone to the dance tonight?" Alan felt uneasy at the line of questioning coming over the line, "I am Sarah… Can you please get me an attorney, um let's see here… David Rosenwood in Glasford?" Alan asked. There was a short pause then she replied, "Yes Deputy…" Alan pulled out the lease agreement while waiting for the line. "Hello, this is the office of David Rosenwood, attorney at law," a young woman said. "May I please talk to Mister Rosenwood? This is Deputy Johnson in Mill Grove," Alan said. "One moment please," came the reply followed by the young woman's muffled voice, "Dad! Someone wants to speak with you."

"Deputy, this is David Rosenwood, how can I help you?" David asked in a cheerful tone. "Mister Rosenwood, I would like to talk with you about Misses Marta Vogal," Alan said. "Yes, I heard about what happened. She was a very nice woman," the lawyer said with concern. "I found papers drawn up by you for the leasing of her farm to James

Palmer. Was there any other work you did for her?" Alan asked.

"I also gave her divorce papers for her daughter Rebecca...," David said. "Did she get them from you on the same day?" Alan asked. "Yes, I sent my secretary to personally deliver them," David said with curiosity. "Mister Rosenwood, I searched the house and could not find the divorce papers," Alan said.

"Well, she got them at the same time. All she needed to do was have Rebecca sign them. I would do the rest of the work," the lawyer said losing his cheerful tone quickly. "So George would not have to sign them?" Alan asked. "No, I would have papers served on him once I had the ones with Rebecca's signature filed with the court," David said. Alan cleared his throat, "So there should be no reason George knew about them?"

"No Deputy, but I think you should know something. Marta was also changing her will. You see, currently if she was to die, her estate would go to Rebecca, but if Rebecca could not accept the estate, it would go to George," David explained. "So in this case George could get her estate and farm?" Alan asked with intrigue. "Well yes, but since he is being charged with her murder, the state will fight any chance of that happening," David said. Alan just processed in his head what was being told to him, "So she was removing George from the will?"

"Yes, that was the proper thing to do since Rebecca was going to divorce him," David said. "Mister Rosenwood, may I ask what else was in her estate besides the farm?" Alan asked smoothly. "She was a wealthy woman, but she did not let it show. I do not think anyone besides her and I knew that fact. Her late husband was a very frugal and smart man. When an investment came along that looked wise, he invested. Misses Vogal had shares in the local grain mill, a foundry in Hazelton and in the interurban line," David said. Alan sat quiet for a few seconds. "Um thank you for your help Mister Rosenwood…," Alan said sounding preoccupied.

Alan hung up the phone to think about what the lawyer said. If Martha had money to live comfortable, why did she force Rebecca to marry George? She could have hired anyone to run the farm and in the end she did. Where were the divorce papers? Did George find them? Did this cause George to kill the women? Alan was getting a headache. In any case he knew that George would be convicted of the murders. There was no other way they could have happened, but Alan did know one fact for sure, there was not one witness to the murder. No one physically saw him pull the trigger and that could be the doubt to sway a jury.

Alan decided to turn his mind to the missing papers from the diary. Just as he opened the desk drawer to retrieve the papers, the door flew open with a young man panting for breath, "Deputy! There is a brawl down at the Rock Wall!

Come quick I think he is going to kill him!" Alan jumped out of his chair and ran toward the door, "Who is going to kill who?" As they exited the building the young man said, "August Palmer and Philip Kiel. Phil was taking out the side of his mouth about the murders and August jumped on him."

The men ran down the street only to see the fight was no longer in the tavern but on the wooden sidewalk outside the door. Both men were bloodied and August was down on the ground with Philip on top. Alan did his best to pull Philip off of August. "Both of you stop! Right now!" Alan grunted as he finally removed Philip. August stood and wiped his bloodied nose with his right wrist. Philip started to walk away. "Get back here. Now!" Alan demanded. Philip Kiel was a large man, about a heads height taller than both Alan and August. "I did nothing wrong… he jumped on me for no reason!" Philip said.

Alan looked to August, "Is that right?" August looked at Philip with an angered face and then looked to Alan, "Yes sir… but he was taking bad about Rebecca!" Alan shook his head, "That is no excuse… What did he say that was so bad?" August looked back to Philip, "He said that his father has already taken care of everything. There is no chance of George even going to trial. He said Rebecca did herself in because she was no woman a man would want…"

Alan looked back at Philip who had a big grin on his face, "Did you say this?" Philip laughed, "It does not matter what I said or did not say… Now I am about to leave because there is nothing you can hold me on… Good-bye deputy…," Philip said then turned to walk away into the crowd of onlookers, "Oh August… you might as well crawl back to your brother… There is no need for your services on my brother's farm." August leaped forward but was caught by Alan, "Calm down damn it!"

August shook free of Alan's grip and watched as Philip walked down the street. "You need to calm down. I cannot have you going off halfcocked right now," Alan said. August looked to see that many of the gawkers were still present. He stepped toward Alan and whispered, "If he gets off deputy… I will kill him with my bare hands…" Alan looked to see the people still standing around, "Everyone go back to what you were doing…" An elderly made is way forward and stated loudly, "He's right you know… George Kiel will walk away. His father has always sheltered that boy." Alan just glared at the man, "No one is walking away from this murder… I will see to that."

August just shook his head in disbelief and reached into his mouth to feel his lower left canine was loose, "Damn… he busted one of my teeth!" Alan gave him a look of disbelief, "You're lucky he did not kill you! He is six inches taller and about fifty pounds heavier! What the hell were you thinking?"

August looked away in shame, "Deputy… Alan… I loved Rebecca with all of my heart and all I think about now is if I would have done something! If only I had told her, maybe she would still be alive right now." Alan shook his head, "Or you both would be dead right now… You need to put your feelings aside right now. Getting into fights with his brother will not help the situation and it will defiantly not bring Rebecca back. By the way, George did not get bail."

August picked his hat up off of the sidewalk and dusted it off. He turned to Alan only to see Charles Kiel's car going by, "Than what the hell is that?!" Alan turned to see George in the passenger's seat. He looked at the men and smiled as the car slowly drove by. "How the hell?" Alan said with an angered tone. He quickly grabbed August by his shirt collar, "come on, let's go make a phone call."

August took off after Alan who was walking at a very swift pace back to his office. Alan flung the door open with enough force to slam it into the wall. He picked up the phone, "Sarah! Sarah!" He paused waiting for the operator to reply. "Get me the States Attorney right now!" August stood next to the desk waiting for Alan's head to explode from his steaming anger.

"This is Deputy Johnson… What? How?" Alan asked with a look of disbelief. "What happened?" August cried only to be quieted by Alan while his eyes rolled from what he was hearing over the phone. "Okay… I have never heard of this happening either… Okay… yes I will keep an eye on the farm… Bye."

Alan hung the phone up and sat down on the top of his desk with a look of shock. "This morning he was refused bail. Somehow a district judge in Chicago overruled Judge Hollingshead and gave George a bond of one hundred dollars," Alan said then shook his head in disbelief. "He murdered two people and was given a bail of one hundred dollars? That amount of money is nothing to his father!" August said as his anger was rebuilding, "So now what?" Alan raised his eyebrow, "They want me to keep an eye on the farm to make sure nothing happens to it until his trial. I will drive you out there to get your things. I believe it would be best for you not to go back there alone."

August sat down on one of the wooden chairs, "He is going to get off… I swear I will…" Alan stopped him, "Shut your mouth and keep your anger under control. I will not let him walk. His father may have money but justice will be served for the women, but it will be done so legally… do you understand?" August just glared back, "Yes… I can go to the farm alone. I will not do anything…" Alan shook his head, "No, I will take you. I am more worried about George or one of his brothers going after you." Alan picked up the phone, "Give your brother a call and ask him to come get you. You can stay here until he arrives."

Chapter 7

Alan went home to get ready for the dance. He took the diary and its missing papers out of his pocket and then placed them on the kitchen table. Amie was now filling his mind and he could finally think of anything but the murders. Alan dressed in his best and only suit. It was a dark tweed that he bought before he moved to Mill Grove from Chicago; however it had only been worn twice in the five years he has owned it. Alan placed the matching hat on his head and looked into the mirror. Being a man, his looks did not mean much to him, unless it came to Amie. He wanted to be polished for her, everything must be perfect. He placed his badge in his pocket, but he locked his gun in his desk drawer for while Alan was always on duty as the local Deputy, tonight he wanted to be a civilian for Amie.

The breeze coming in the car did little to cool Alan as he sweltered in the heat on his way to the Lynch farm. He pulled into their driveway trying to miss the occasional chicken who stumbled into the path of the REO. The well taken care of house sat on a slight hill overlooking the road and Martha Vogal's farm. Alan walked to the front porch to knock on the door, but first turned around to look where the murders took place. You can see the farmhouse and its property with an almost completely unobstructed view except for a few trees in the front yard. You could see the house, the barn yard and the kitchen porch. If Kenneth Lynch was sitting in his doorway as he said, he should have seen everything. He should have heard the shots, but he said he was unaware of the situation until George came running for help.

Alan turned his attention back to the front door. He was so nervous, scared almost, he felt like a small child going to school for the first time. He took deep, slow breaths trying to calm himself. Alan looked to the left of the front door to see a small wooden chair. Alan imagined this was the chair that Ken was sitting on that day. He again looked back to the farm, but reality came back quickly, it was time to take the woman he loved to the dance and quit thinking about murder.

Turning once again to the door, Alan raised his hand to knock. Just as his knuckles made contact with the door, it flew open with Kenneth Lynch glaring at back. "Well are you going to come in or stand there all night?" Ken barked. Alan stood silent for a second thinking of what to say. "Umm… hello Mister Lynch," Alan said like a lost child. Ken's face stayed still like a tombstone when he stated with a reluctant monotone, "Alan, please come in. Amie is still getting ready."

Alan walked in taking note of his surroundings. "Please sit here," Ken said as he motioned his hand to the couch in the parlor. "Thank you," Alan said while sitting down. Ken proceeded to sit down in a well-worn parlor chair.

Both men stared at one another not wanting to be the one to say the first word. Alan's stomach was starting to burn from his thoughts of the hatred Ken must have for him. No one would be good enough for Amie in Ken's eyes Alan was thinking to himself. A fly was buzzing around the room but left quickly as if it felt the tension between the men.

They sat for three minutes in silence looking for any subject to speak on. "Alan… I saw that you arrested George," Ken said trying to find anything to talk about. "Yes," Alan gave quickly and with little effort. "So he killed Rebecca?" Ken asked. "Yes, we believe so. The case is still developing…," Alan said.

"I see…," Ken said. Alan could tell at this moment he is holding something back. "Mister Lynch, can you please tell me what happened that day?" Alan asked slipping back into his profession. "I already told you. I was on the porch and George can running saying he was shot by Rebecca," Ken stated with a slightly angered tone. "Is there anything else you would like to tell me?" Alan asked. "What else is there to say?" Ken said with his voice becoming more cross.

"Ken… Mister Lynch, I need your help. You were on the front porch with a good view of the house. While I know you cannot see inside, you have a good view of the outside. You must have seen something. You must have heard the shots," Alan said; his tone becoming sharp.

From across the room came a creak of the wooden floor that startled the men. "What are you two talking about?" Amie said while standing in the vestibule next to the parlor. She was wearing a white dress; her blonde hair pulled back into a bun. Alan lost all thought with the first sight of the woman he loved, but didn't even notice her mother and her sister were standing with her. Alan stood up from the couch, removed his hat, but was completely speechless by her beauty. "Alan, I hope you were not talking about the murders, I was hoping we would have the night to us, not the Kiel's," Amie said gently.

"Oh, we were just talking, as men do," Alan said with a smile while not removing his eyes from Amie's beauty. Ken looked to Alan with a clinched jaw. "Besides, you can talk with father all you want tomorrow. Mother has invited you to dinner," Amie said with a smile. "Dinner?" Ken said before stopping himself. "Dinner… why that will be great," Alan said feeling his stomach knotting even tighter. "You two better be moving on," Misses Lynch said, "I hope you two will have a nice night." Alan looked to a Grandfather clock next to the stairs, "Oh, yes, we better get going. It is getting late."

Alan walked toward Amie, but Ken abruptly stopped him by placing his left hand on Alan's chest. "Please have her back at a respectable hour Alan," Ken said in a stern voice. "Oh, I will sir," Alan said feeling very small in Ken's presence. "Remember Sunday dinner also. How about two o'clock?" Misses Lynch asked. "Yes, two, that will be very nice," Alan said with reassurance. He took Amie's hand and escorted her out to his car. The air was stuffy and the buzz of insects was loud but it was all good for Alan, for he had Amie by the hand.

Alan opened the car door for Amie and helped her into the car. He carefully closed the door behind her and went to start the car. Alan pulled a white silk handkerchief out of his breast pocket so he would not get grease on his hands from the crank. The car was slow to start, but finally it took off. Alan prayed that Ken did not notice the resistance the engine was giving him. Alan stood up straight, placed the handkerchief in his pants pocket and walked as if on air to the driver's door. As he sat in the car, he looked back toward the house to see Misses Lynch looking proud at her daughter in the front seat. Kenneth however looked like the executioner waiting for his next victim.

It was seven o'clock but the sun was still high in the western sky as they drove into town. Every move Alan made was calculated as he did not want to embarrass himself in front of Amie. "So dinner tomorrow night…," Alan said. "Yes, you do want to come?" Amie asked. "Oh, yes, I cannot wait," Alan replied with a smile. "Alan, I know my father worries you, but please be understanding of him. He just worries about me," Amie said as she placed her hand on Alan's right leg. "I know Amie," Alan said.

The town hall was the original schoolhouse for Mill Grove. It was a simple wood framed building with one large room on the first floor and a large basement that held the offices for the mayor and other functions of the town. The city council would use the room upstairs, but the tables were removed so dances could take place and other events. The summer dance was an important function for the town. This would be one of the last times everyone would come together before the harvesting would start for the variety of crops that grew in the surrounding areas. The next dance of the year would not be until late October, that was the harvest dance and it would celebrate the last of the crops being harvested.

Alan parked as close as he could to the front stairs of the town hall. It was one of only three automobiles to be attending the dance. Everyone else came on wagons or rode horses into town. Alan stepped out of the car and swiftly went to help Amie out. Instantly they could smell food coming from the hall and hear the sounds of the band warming up. Amie and Alan walked into the hall to see many of the townspeople were already in attendance. Some were dressed in their best clothes, but others were dressed like another day on the farm. In any case they all came to eat, have fun and dance.

Alan was proud to have Amie on his arm; he felt she was the most beautiful woman in town and in most instances, she was. As they walked in, the chatter of the people quieted down. Alan could feel everyone looking at him, was it because of Amie? Was it because of the murders? His unknotted stomach had just retightened itself.

The young couple went to the west wall of the hall and found two chairs to sit on. "Alan, I think everyone has the same thing on their minds," Amie said quietly into his left ear. "Yes, this was the biggest news this town has seen in years," Alan replied. Alan looked back up to the crowd to see Mayor Hines coming toward him with two members of the town council. "Deputy," the mayor said, "may we please speak with you about the Kiel incident?" Alan looked up to the men and said in a polite tone, "Mayor, please see me Monday morning. Tonight I want to keep my attention on Amie." The mayor looked back at Alan shocked, but then saw the beautiful woman sitting next to him, "Very well deputy, but we must talk about the repercussions these murders may have on our community." Alan smiled, "Do not worry, on Monday we will talk… Good night mayor, gentlemen."

The mayor and the council members walked back into the crowd angered. "Alan, I hope you will not be in trouble," Amie said. "I am not worried, besides I told them the truth, tonight is about you, not murder." Alan said then kissed Amie on her temple.

The band started to play a slow song to get the night started. Quickly the dance floor opened up for those who wanted to dance. "Would you like to dance my dear?" Alan asked with a flirtatious tone. "Why yes Mister Johnson, I would love to," Amie said with a smile while she started to walk out onto the floor. Alan was not the best at dancing, but he tried hard. It really did not matter that Alan was not the best dancer; Amie was in love and could not care one bit about his clumsiness. This dance would be first of many that night.

They took their position on the light oak floor with five other couples. The song was slow, sweet. Alan placed his hands just above Amie's hips as she wrapped her arms around his neck. They were close, but were not married, so they kept a distance between their bodies. Alan tried to lead, but she was the one who knew the moves. As they danced Alan looked into her eyes, he smelled her perfume. He was a man in love and Amie was the woman he waited his whole life for.

The first dance went well but only lasted three minutes before it came to an abrupt stop when the guitar player broke two strings at the same time. "Sorry everyone, we will be back in shape in a few minutes. In the meantime please help yourself to some great food and refreshments," the singer said in a gruff tone. Alan held his stance as if in a trance. "Um, Alan. Why don't we go get some food? I'm hungry," Amie said as she removed her hands from his shoulders. Alan shook his head in agreement but was slow to remove his hands from her waist. Before he removed his hands, he tightened his grip slightly and moved his thumbs in a sweeping movement. Amie winked at him and gave a thin smile.

At the back of the room were tables draped with checkered table cloths. They contained the food for the dance and the locals were quickly cleaning the bowls and plates. Alan and Amie walked over to see the feeding frenzy. "Maybe we should just go to the restaurant and I can make us something," Amie said in amazement. "No, no. There is enough here for everyone… I think," Alan said with a chuckle, "why don't you go grab a place for us to sit and I will wrestle for the food." Amie laughed and shook her head in agreement, "Sure, just be careful you do not lose a limb."

Amie sat down at an empty table with six chairs around it perimeter. She watched as her boyfriend did his best to balance two plates on one arm and move around the feeding frenzy. Her attention was quickly changed when she overheard a group of people behind her speaking of the murder that week.

Alan placed the plates on the table but before he could sit a man walked out from the group behind Amie. "Deputy I need to speak with you, alone," the white haired man said with a tone of urgency. Alan looked to Amie who just rolled her eyes. "Yes Sir, let's go out onto the steps." Alan said, "I will be right back Honey." Amie gave a blank look and then picked up her fork to taste her dinner. The men made their way through the crowd and walked through the wooden entrance doors. "Okay, what do you need to tell me?" Alan asked with a cross tone. The man looked around to see no one was around them, "You need to know… they are talking about getting a lynching party together." Alan gave a look of anger, "Lynch who?" The man looked out to the dark street and said in a soft tone, "Who do you think? George Kiel!"

Alan stepped back and leaned against the pipe railing. "Who is saying this?" Alan asked. The man shook his head and said, "I do not know. I just have heard around town this afternoon that he was out of jail. Many people are angry," the man said in a soft voice. "I do not recognize you, what is your name sir?" Alan asked with an angered tone. "You do not know me and you do not need to know my name. You do need to know those murders are splitting this town into two camps. It will not take long before the anger boils over," the man said as he stepped forward to Alan. "Well now you have told me and I am going back into the dance," Alan said then reached for the handle of one of the doors.

The man grabbed Alan's left arm, "It is your duty to protect this town, everyone in this town." Alan looked down to the man's hand, "I know my job mister and I do it damn well. I am not George Kiel's bodyguard however. If you are so concerned about his safety, go drive out to his farm." Alan opened the door and walked back into the dance leaving the man on the steps.

Alan sat at the table to see his love sitting with an expressionless face. "What was that all about?" Amie asked. Alan picked up a fork and dug into some potato salad. "Just someone who is concerned that a civil war is about to break out," Alan said with a chuckle. Amie raised her right eyebrow and asked, "Civil war?" Alan swallowed his first taste of the potato salad and said, "He heard that a lynch party is being organized. They all want to lynch George Kiel…" Amie looked around to see some people at the next table were listening in. She leaned over and said to Alan, "Let's forget about the murder for the rest of the evening. Okay?" Alan shook his head in agreement but did not say a word due to the large amount of food in his mouth.

The young couple tried their best to talk while they enjoyed the dinner and the music the band was playing. With every word Alan would say he would notice people trying to overhear. Alan moved his chair as close to Amie as he could then leaned in to whisper into her ear, "Why does everyone want to know what I am saying to you?" Amie giggled, "Because the only way people learn anything in this town is through gossip. I guess they think you are full of it… gossip I mean…" Alan started to laugh, "I'm glad you clarified that statement!"

Alan went to take a bite of watermelon when he stopped, pulled in close to Amie once again and whispered into her ear, "Do you want to have a little fun with the people?" Amie smiled and shook her head in agreement. Alan pulled back, took a bite of the watermelon and said in a not so soft whisper, "Do you know who Jimmy White is?" Amie paused, "Um, yes, he comes into the restaurant on occasion." Alan peered over with just his eyes to see a few couples were listening in on the conversation, "Well I arrested him yesterday... seems he liked to look into women's windows." Amie gasped, "Really?" Alan shook his head, "Yes and well, the reason I arrested him was because he liked to steal their... well, I shouldn't mention them in mixed company." Amie tried her best not to laugh, "So what will happen to him?" Alan carefully looked around to see that more people were listening, "I took him into Glasford where the judge ordered him sent to the institution in Elgin... So now that we have a little energy, let's go dance some more."

Alan stood, took Amie by the hand and led her onto the dance floor just in time for a new song to start. As Alan took her back into his arms Amie asked, "Who is Jimmy White?" Alan laughed, "Hell if I know. Let's move around a bit as we dance and see if the gossip is flowing yet." Amie giggled and said, "I wonder if the story will be in Monday's paper?" Alan smiled largely, "Oh I hope so!"

In Amie's and Alan's eyes, the night went by in a flash. They could have danced the whole night away and tell some more tall tales to flame the town gossip. The band was winding down on their last song when Alan looked around to see that they were the only couple left on the floor. The remaining couples were either sitting and chatting or getting ready to leave. "I guess it is time to go…" Amie said in a quiet tone. "Yes, I guess so… I must get you back at a respectable time," Alan said joking. "Yes, my father will be waiting I am sure," Amie said with a big smile.

When the band stopped the couple held one another and did not let go. Alan took Amie closer to his body, held her tight and kissed her in a way he never did before. At that moment time stood still for the young couple. Alan slowly pulled away and opened his eyes to see that Amie's eyes were closed. In a soft whisper he said, "Amie I love you."

They went home that night having feelings stronger for one another than they have every felt. Alan stopped the car in front of her house and helped Amie out. Alan was hoping to have one more kiss for the night, but that was shattered by Kenneth opening the door. "Well deputy, it is not too late," Ken said, "I am sure you two had a nice evening….." Alan looked at Amie with a smile. "Oh yes father, I had a wonderful time," Amie said walking into the house. Alan was following her in, but was stopped quickly. "We will see you tomorrow afternoon for dinner, deputy," Ken stated dryly as he placed himself between Alan and the door. "Oh, yes see you tomorrow afternoon at two. Please have a nice night Amie," Alan said. "Good night Alan…," Amie returned as her father was closing the door.

Alan turned around and looked up into the darkness of the night. The stars were bright through the summer haze and the moon was rising over the horizon. It all, it was a wonderful night. He walked down the steps to his car to see that an oil lamp was lit in the parlor of farmhouse across the road. At that moment he remembered Amie's request to forget about the murders for the evening.

Chapter 8

"I have held a heavy heart this past week. I have seen the work of the Devil in our tiny hamlet. It was his hand on the trigger of the gun that took the lives of two beautiful, loving women! It is also his work in the fractions I see our community splitting into! Talk is on the street of lawlessness coming to our town… and many of the faces of those sitting before me show the signs of anger and distress. Only God will judge the wicked, it is not ours to do his work. Now, let us pray…"

Alan was sitting in the last pew of the Saint John's Lutheran Church trying not to doze off from his late night at the dance. Thankfully Pastor Travis Crawford's fiery sermon has kept him attentive. Alan does not attend church often but felt it may be a good place to be seen. Sitting five rows in front of him was the Lynch family. Three rows in front of them were Charles Kiel and his family. However missing from the clan was George. Alan was not surprised by this and was happy not to see him.

When mass was over, Pastor Crawford took his normal position on the front steps of the white clapboarded church thanking each member of the flock as they exited the building. Alan sat and watched the people leave. It was quite clear that as the pastor spoke of, the town's people were splitting into two camps, those who knew George committed the act of murder and those who think a Kiel could never do wrong.

Amie passed by wearing a simple black dress, her golden blonde hair French braided. As she passed she gave a smile and wink to Alan who happily smiled back. Unfortunately for Alan, Kenneth spotted the smile toward his eldest daughter. He did not smile for Alan; in fact he did not make any expression at all. That spoke volumes to Alan.

Alan took to his feet, picked up his hat from his side and walked toward the doors. As he walked out in the morning sun, Pastor Crawford stepped forward and took a commanding pose in front of the deputy. "Deputy Johnson... it is indeed an honor to have you present this morning. I cannot remember the last time I had the honor," the pastor said sharply. Alan sought for the proper words, "I felt with the sorrow our community has experienced recently, a visit to the church would be in order for my soul." The pastor raised his right eyebrow and said, "If you soul needs mending, it is not a process that can happen with just one visit to church. It takes time and devotion... one sermon does not show devotion to the Lord."

Alan did his best to hold his composure, "Well Pastor, it was a good sermon. I will see you next Sunday morning for sure." Alan placed his hat on his head and started to walk down the granite steps. "I understand you were not happy with me when I did not allow Melissa Kiel admission to the cemetery. Killing one's self only buys admission to the table of the damned…," the pastor stated dryly. Alan turned around to face the pastor now two feet higher in the air. "Pastor, she did not kill herself. She is an innocent victim and the only table she is at presently… is with the Lord," Alan said sharply. The pastor stepped down to look Alan in the eye, "Have you not seen your investigation is doing nothing more that splitting this community. The women are dead, let them rest in peace."

"Two women were murdered. Do you not want the person who took their lives held accountable for his actions?" Alan asked. "It is not man's duty to pass judgment on his fellow man; the Lord will pass judgment when the murderer stands before him. What you are doing is ruining the name of one of this county's finest families. Take my advice deputy, let this case lie before this town is in flames," the pastor retorted then walked back to the doors of the church. "What is it about the Kiel family, Pastor?" Alan asked.

The pastor stopped and turned around to the inquisitive deputy, "What do you mean?" Alan walked back up the steps, "Why do you feel the need to protect them?" The pastor opened his mouth only to shut it quickly. He paused for a second then said in a mellow tone, "I am not protecting them. I only feel you need to realize they are not the evil you portray them to be. Now, I have work to do and I am sure you do also. Good day."

Alan looked at the pastor to see the anger he was trying to hold back and said, "The storm last summer..." The pastor squinted his eyes and asked, "What about it?" Alan looked up to the steeple then back to the pastor, "The church was damaged by the whirlwind; the steeple took severe damage and most of the shingles were sucked off. You had a bake sale to raise funds but it was a donation that provided the funds; one large donation... Charles Kiel I assume?"

The pastor removed a handkerchief from his pocket and wiped the sweat from the back of his neck. "Yes Mister Kiel was very sympathetic to our cause and very helpful," he stated with ease. "When you spoke in your sermon about the town splitting, I thought you were speaking as an impartial party. It appears you were speaking more to those who believe that George Kiel committed murder," Allan stated with purpose. The pastor stepped forward, placed himself very close to Alan's face and said with his fiery sermon tone, "If there is anyone who is showing how impartial he is not, it is you... Good day!"

Alan watched the pastor walk into the church and with great force, slammed the doors behind him. Alan turned to see a small group of the town's people that had witnessed the very vivid argument between the two men. Alan walked down the steps, then across the church lawn to avoid the people. It was beyond him why some people would hold the Kiel family with honor usually only afforded to royalty.

Alan stepped onto the porch of his house to find the Sunday newspaper. He looked down on the front page to see the announcement of George Kiel being given bail. What was missing from the article was that it took a group of lawyers and a judge to overrule the revocation of bond. Alan threw the paper on the kitchen table and opened up a kitchen cupboard. He pulled out a pack of Lucky Strike cigarettes and a silver lighter. He lit a cigarette, walked out onto the back porch and sat on an old wooden chair. "I wonder if it is worth finding who killed the women," he said out loud to the hazy midday sun. He relaxed as he smoked his anger and stress away. As the cigarette burned away, Alan drifted to sleep in the comfortable chair.

The sound of a hawk caused Alan to wake from his trance and look to his watch to see that it was almost one o'clock, "I better get ready for dinner." Alan looked to see his cigarette was about burned to his fingers. He took one last drag then threw the butt to the lawn. As he exhaled the smoke, he walked into the house.

Alan entered the kitchen and placed the lighter back into the cabinet. As he went to wash up he looked down to the newspaper on the kitchen table. Next to it was the diary and the missing pages. Alan picked up the book, pulled out the found pages and glanced them over. "More of the same crap…

these pages are useless," Alan said out loud in anger, "I cannot believe I wasted my time looking for them." Alan placed them back into the diary with little regard and threw the diary onto the table.

Alan took a longer path to the Lynch farm. He did not want to pass the Kiel farm and wished he did not have to see the Vogal farm. The crops were doing well and the corn was growing at a faster pace than normal. The dirt roads seemed like brown valleys among mountains of green. Alan could not see past the stalks and each intersection was an exercise in caution to avoid hitting another vehicle or animal. As Alan turned onto the gravel path leading to the Lynch farm he looked over to the Vogal farm. Sitting on the kitchen porch was George with a bottle in his hand. Alan just shook his head in disbelief of the sight.

Alan slowed down his car with a screech. "Got to get those brakes fixed," Alan said out loud. Kenneth was sitting on the porch of the farmhouse; his Sunday brown suit was replaced by his everyday denim overalls and a white cotton shirt. He barely took his eyes off of the stick he was whittling when Alan parked the car in front of the house.

"What are you making?" Alan asked as he walked up on to the porch. Ken carefully looked at the piece, took another pass with his knife then said, "I do not know yet, just started a few minutes ago." Alan sat on a stool and watched Ken work. "What do you normally whittle?" Alan asked. Ken stopped for a second then took another pass, "Anything I want I guess, been doing this for years… gotten pretty good at it."

Alan could hear the sounds of women laughing and plates being set on the table. He turned his attention back to Ken as a way of hopefully easing Ken's thoughts of him. "When did you learn your hobby?" Alan asked with a sense of curiosity. Ken placed the knife down and looked to Alan, "It was Amie's first Christmas. Grace and I were poor, very poor. Crops that year failed and we barely had enough money to make rent on the land. Grace saw a porcelain doll in the general store and wanted to give it to Amie. There was no way we could afford it so I decided to carve one. Grace made clothes for it out of some scraps of old fabric. It didn't turn out too bad. Amie still has it, says she wants to give it to her daughter."

Alan did not know what to say after Ken's last sentence. "Well, I will have to ask Amie to see it," Alan said trying to find a way to change the subject. Ken picked his knife back up and started to work on the stick again, "It's in her bedroom and you will not be seeing that anytime soon, deputy." Alan stayed quiet with this latest statement. The creak of the wood floor behind him almost caused Alan to shoot off of the stool.

"Alan, I did not know you are here…," Amie said with surprise. "Yes he has been learning how to whittle," Ken said swiftly as he peered down the stick with precision. "Dinner will be ready in a few minutes. Mom wanted me to tell you to wash up pa," Amie said cheerfully. Ken looked up at his eldest daughter with a look of displeasure. He stood up, placed the stick and knife on the chair then walked into the house.

Amie watched her father pass into the house and peered through the doorway to make sure he completed his journey to the kitchen. "What's this about my bedroom?" Amie asked with a flirtatious tone. "Oh... nothing. He told me about a doll he made you when you will little," Alan said with a small smile. Amie sat on Alan's lap and placed her left arm on back of his neck. Alan moved his face in a way that his nose brushed lightly against her now unbraided hair. Its light flowery smell was causing Alan's heart to beat faster and his breathing to deepen.

Amie turned to look at Alan when she could tell his mood was changing. "I had a nice time last night," Amie said. "I did also. I wished the night would have never ended," Alan said then went to kiss Amie on the lips. Just as their lips touched came the sound of a very large, imposing man clearing his throat. "Dinner is on the table," Ken said in a very gruff tone then turned around and walked back into the house. Amie's eyes were big from the quick interruption, but it did not stop Alan from stealing one last kiss.

Alan pulled back from Amie to see her eyes were closed just like last night. "I guess we better get inside," Alan said softly. Amie opened her eyes slowly then hugged him snugly. Before she let go, she whispered into his ear, "I never told you last night. I love you also." Alan wrapped his arms around her waist and pulled her tight. "I've been waiting my whole life for you," Alan said in a whisper. "We are going to eat without both of you!" came Ken's voice soaring from inside the house.

Sunday dinner was a very important event in the Lynch household and Alan knew his invitation was very important to his future with Amie. They walked into the dining room to see Ken sitting at the head of the table carving the ham. Robin and her mother, Grace, were sitting at Kens right. Alan pulled out the chair closest to Ken and motioned to Amie to sit. "So formal," Amie said as he slid the chair in for her as she sat.

"Alan, I hope you like ham," Grace said. Alan looked at all of the food on the table, "Yes, I love ham Misses Lynch. There is so much food… This is like Thanksgiving in July." Ken rolled his eyes as he placed a piece of ham on his wife's plate. "Please call me Grace, no need to be so formal," Grace said as she reached for a biscuit. Robin spooned a heap of mashed potatoes on her plate then slipped into the conversation, "I saw George Kiel drinking on his porch last night…"

Ken placed his fork onto his plate with a heavy hand, "Two minutes into the meal and you had to bring that man up!" Grace placed her hand on Ken's to calm him and said, "Robin, dinner is not an appropriate place to talk about the Kiel's." Robin looked to her mother then to Alan, "I thought the law is here to protect us from criminals? Why is he back right across the road from us?" Alan did not know how to respond to the verbal assault. "Robin stop!" Ken said firmly. She looked to her father then held her tongue from what she wanted to say.

"Why don't we find another subject," Amie said in hopes of calming the growing tempers. "Yes that's a good idea. Um, did you enjoy Pastor Crawford's sermon this morning, Alan?" Grace asked. Before Alan could respond Robin spoke up and asked, "What was in the diary deputy?" Ken looked to his younger daughter, "What diary?" Alan could feel the tension growing to a dangerous climax, "Um, Rebecca Kiel's diary." Ken looked to Alan with more distaste than normal, "Why does my youngest daughter know about a dead woman's diary?" The diners sat quiet until Amie responded, "Robin gave it to Alan... Misses Kiel asked her to keep it for her."

Ken stood up from his chair, "I am sick and tired of hearing about the Kiel family! Now I find out that my youngest daughter held a diary for a dead woman?" Grace looked up to her husband, "Honey, sit down and let's try to have a nice dinner.

Please, we have a guest…" Ken looked over to Alan, "Yes our guest, the great policeman who is trying to steal my oldest daughter from me. Deputy, let me ask you one question… if you cannot keep a murderer behind bars, how the hell can I trust you to take care of my daughter?"

Alan was trying his best to keep his temper in check, "Sir, the love I have for your daughter is stronger that any law or judge. I cannot control a rich father throwing money around to save his son but I will not be told that I cannot protect the woman I love. Amie I am sorry, but perhaps I should leave." Grace reached across the table, "Please Alan, stay. Girls your father had an announcement he was going to make. Ken, please tell them the good news."

Ken took his stare off of Alan and slowly sat back down into his chair. "What did you want to tell us dad?" Amie asked. Ken took a sip of his water then reached under his napkin for an envelope. "We have had some good years recently. Your mother and I have tried our best to save our money. Yesterday I paid off the mortgage on the farm nine years early," Ken said proudly, his tone changed from just a few seconds prior, "The farm is fully ours now."

Amie looked to her mother then to her father, "I did not know you were saving that much money? This is great news… finally we have something good to talk about." Robin looked at her sister then to her father, "Well since we are doing so good, do we have money to send me to college when I graduate next year?" Grace looked over to Robin, "If you want to go to college we will do what we can." Ken did not say a word but the smile he had a heartbeat earlier was now erased.

Alan listened as the family talked over their good news. It was occurring to him that he had just declared before an entire family the love he holds for one of its members. He remained quiet eating his meal for fear of saying anything that could kick off another family feud.

When the meal was finished Alan went into the parlor as the women cleaned the table. Ken sat silently in his chair looking at Alan. When the grandfather clock chimed to announce it was four o'clock Ken did not say a word nor change his posture. "We have coffee and chocolate cake for dessert," Amie announced as she entered the silent room. Alan stood up from his chair to walk to the dining room as Ken remained quiet. Alan followed Amie toward the dining room leaving Ken behind.

"What have you two been talking about?" Amie whispered. "Nothing. He has been sitting stone faced. Amie, he really hates me, doesn't he?" Alan asked. "No he does not hate you Alan," Grace said as she pour coffee into cups, "I think age is starting to catch up with him. His little girls are no longer little and they are both eager to start their own lives." Ken walked into the room, took a cup of coffee and walked out to the kitchen porch. "I didn't know dad was saving up to pay off the mortgage. He should be so happy right now," Amie said. Grace took a sip of the coffee then reached for a sugar cube, "Truthfully I did not know either. Since he handles the money, I do not know much of what our finances are. Now, how about some cake Alan?"

Chapter 9

Alan sat at the counter eating a plate of scrambled eggs while watching Amie serving the tables in the restaurant. "It's one busy morning," Amie stated as she swiftly passed Alan with a coffee pot. Many people were in the restaurant this morning and with Amie being the only waitress, Alan has not been able to speak much with her. He slowly ate his breakfast hoping for the restaurant to quiet down.

His plate was cleared and his cup was dry as the crowd slowly dissipated. "I cannot believe how busy we were this morning," Amie said as she sat on a stool next to Alan, "would you like anything else to eat?" Alan looked at his plate and then back to Amie, "No I am good." Amie reached down and rubbed her right ankle, "I am beat already. I hope the rest of the day will be slow. So… we have not spoken yet about yesterday's dinner." Alan raised his eyebrow and asked cautiously, "What are you referring to?" Amie giggled, "Let's say mother and me had a very long conversation about you last night."

Alan picked up his coffee cup for a sip only to find it empty. "Here, I will get you more," Amie said as she reached for the coffee pot. She filled his cup and placed the pot down. Alan slowly took a sip. "What did she say about me?" Alan asked while looking down into his cup. "She thinks you are a nice man and dad will warm up to you… in time," Amie said. Alan looked up to see a smile on her face.

"Alan… did you mean what you said yesterday?" Amie asked. Alan reached over and took her left hand into his, "Yes, very much so. I know I do not tell you how much you mean to me. Sometimes men have a hard time expressing their feelings." Amie squeezed his hand then reached over and hugged him. "Alan I love you very, very much," she said softly. Alan pulled his head away and kissed Amie gently on her lips. "I love you too Honey," he said softly.

"Alan, do you hear a bell ringing?" Amie asked. Alan pulled away and listened, "That's the fire bell. I better get going and find out what is going on, ten dollars says the chief is drunk again... I will be back for lunch." Amie started to laugh, "Look at the clock, it's after ten!" Alan put his hat on and walked to the door only to turn around. "Amie" he said, "I love you." Amie smiled, "I love you too, Alan."

Alan turned and walked out to the sidewalk to see men racing out of town on their horses and some others in their automobiles. "Deputy!" a man shouted from his horse, "there is a fire at the Vogal farm. You better come." Amie was standing in the doorway just in time to hear what the man said. "Alan, what if it is really our farm?!" Amie asked with worry. "I'm sure it's nothing Honey. I will let you know what happened when I come back later," Alan said with a reassuring tone.

Alan started his car, jumped in and waved back to Amie as he started down the road. He was not far out of town when he could see black smoke billowing out into the hazy sky. He arrived at the Vogal farm to see the farm house fully engulfed by flames. The local farmers and their families had organized bucket brigades and were trying to stop the flames. He parked his car on the edge of the road and jumped out to help.

"Has anyone see George Kiel?" Alan asked of the people running with buckets of water. No one answered as they were too busy to worry. Alan saw that the house started to fall in on itself unleashing clouds of smoke and embers. "Start wetting down the barn!" came a voice from the crowd. The town's volunteer firemen were beginning to move the people back as it was a lost battle to save the house. The families went back to the road exhausted from their fight and unhappy with the loss.

The fire chief, Isaac Wooten, was the last to walk away from the holocaust; his clothes and face cover with soot. "Isaac, have you seen George Kiel?" Alan asked with urgency. "No deputy, I have not seen him. If he was still inside, he did not make it," the chief said during bouts of coughing. "Here, take some water," Grace Lynch said to the chief while holding a bucket with a steel ladle. The chief took the ladle and cleared his cough with cold water. "Grace, have you seen George?" Alan asked. "No Alan… his father is helping Kenneth pump the well," Grace said with a somber tone.

Alan walked up the driveway to find Ken and Charles Kiel sitting on the edge of a wooden trough next to the wellhead. "Mister Lynch, Mister Kiel… Have either of you seen George?" Alan asked. Charles remained silent, his vision fixed upon the site of the burning house. "No one has seen him deputy," Ken said. "Were you first to see the fire?" Alan asked Ken. "Yes I went out to the barn and could smell something burning. I came out to find what it was, that's when I saw flames coming from the house," Ken stated, "I jumped on my horse and rode to Charles' farm, he has the closest telephone."

Charles sat quiet listening to the men talk and watching what was left of the house crumbling into glowing masses of flame and clouds of embers. "Mister Kiel when was the last time you spoke with George?" Alan asked. Charles looked up at Alan then turned back to watching the house burn. "Saturday afternoon," Charles said quietly, "he a… he wanted to be left alone. So I brought him back here when we returned from Glasford."

Alan finally saw the side of Charles Kiel many do not see. He was no longer the hard driving land owner; he was a man whose heart was grieving the loss of a son. "When the flames are out the coroner will remove the… will removed George,"

118

Alan said, "I will go back and contact him now." Charles did not acknowledge what Alan said and sat quietly watching the flames.

The afternoon humidity was giving way to rounds of thunderstorms that pounded the town with high winds and rain. Alan and Coroner Knight arrived at the burned-out farmhouse as the late afternoon sun was reemerging from behind the clouds. "Here we are again," the coroner said as the remains of the house came into view. The men walked to what was earlier the Vogal farmhouse. The only visible signs left of the house were the fieldstone foundation and chimney.

"Where do we begin?" Alan asked with astonishment. "Do you have a shovel in your automobile?" the coroner asked. Alan shook his head, "No. I will look out in the barn, I am sure there are tools we can use." Alan walked to the barn and slid open the weathered wooden door. Inside was a rack holding shovels, pitch forks and rakes. Alan grabbed two shovels and a pitch fork then walked back to the foundation.

"Well I will start on that end and you can start on this end deputy," the coroner said as he surveyed the remains of the house. Small wisps of white smoke were still rising in the air from the ashes. Alan walked down stone steps that lead to the root cellar under what was the kitchen. Among the burned pieces of lumber were shattered mason jars,

119

the cast iron kitchen stove and various kitchen utensils. Alan moved the ashes around but nothing looked like human remains. '

"I saw you two over here, I thought you would need some help," Ken said as he stood at the edge of the foundation holding a shovel in his right hand. Alan looked up from the pit, "Yes any help would be appreciated." Ken took a stance in the middle of the two men and started to dig in with vengeance. He really did not know what he was looking for but felt he would know it when he found it.

The sun was lowering into the western sky as the men continued to work. "Why don't we break for the day and go at this in the morning. We do not have much light left to work with," the coroner said, his soot covered face gave the look of an actor ready for a minstrel show. Alan turned to agree with the coroner when something looked out of place in front of him. He knelt down and moved broken pieces of glass. "Coroner Knight, I think I found George," Alan said with a somber tone.

The coroner walked around to the steps and proceeded down into the root cellar. Ken kept his stance but stopped shoveling. The coroner knelt down next to Alan and carefully moved a piece of debris. "Proximal, intermediate, and distal phalanges," the coroner said in a monotone. "What the hell is that?" Ken asked feeling very uneducated. "Finger bones Mister Lynch. The rest of him must be under these beams… Mister Lynch, can you fetch a couple lanterns?" the coroner asked. "Yes I will be right back," Ken said. The coroner pulled up a piece of burned wood to expose more of George's arm, "It appears he was down here during the fire. These are the support beams for the first floor. If he was upstairs he would be above them, not below."

Alan stood up and went to the other side of charred beams. "I can see the rest of the skeleton I believe," Alan said just as Ken returned with two lanterns. "Here, I also brought a pry bar with," Ken said. Alan took the lanterns from Ken and placed them on steel hooks that extended out of the fieldstone wall. "Both of you stand over on this side with me. We will use the pry bar to remove the beam," the coroner said as he stood to his feet.

Ken placed the pry bar at the foot of the beam, its head lying in a pocket of the fieldstone wall. Ken lifted up on the beam with a grunt, but it barely moved. "Alan, give me a hand," Ken said. Alan grabbed the bar on the opposing side from Ken. "Ready," Alan said. "Okay, now," Ken said. This time the beam moved enough to the side that the coroner could remove the rest of the remains. The coroner knelt down and felt around under the skull, its color a reddish black. "What is that?" Alan said with curiosity. The coroner looked up to Alan, "It appears to be rope." Ken looked at the coroner, "Rope?"

Alan took the pry bar and threw it on the ground outside of the foundation. "I would have never thought he would be one to kill himself," Alan said in disbelief. "I guess the guilt of what he did got to him," the coroner said, "can you fetch the leather bag from the automobile deputy?" Ken started to walk to the steps, "I will get it… I um… need some air." Ken walked up the steps to see Amie and Robin standing nearby. "How long have you two been here?" Ken asked of his daughters. "Long enough to hear that he took his own life," Amie said. "Why don't you two go back to the house… This is not a place for young women to be," Ken stated sternly. Robin shook her head and turned toward their house. "We have dinner for all of you when you are ready," Amie said. "That sounds good Honey," came Alan's voice from the root cellar.

Ken grabbed the leather bag and took it down to the men. "We will place the bones in the bag and deliver them to the funeral home. There is really nothing for me to do. It is quite obvious what happened here this morning," the coroner stated as he opened the leather bag, "when I return to Glasford in the morning I will notify the state's attorney. I cannot speak for him, but I believe the murder case will now be closed since the prime suspect is dead by his own hand."

Alan started to help the coroner by picking the bones up and placing them in the back. He placed his hands on the skull but it quickly slipped out of his grip due to the few remaining pieces of unburned flesh. Alan's stomach made a deep growl. "Deputy, if you are going to be sick, I ask that you do it out in the yard… preferably out of ear range," the coroner said as he picked up the skull and placed it in the bag. "I'm fine, just hungry I guess," Alan said. "You're hungry? Jesus Christ…," Ken said in a shocked tone.

Alan stood up and pushed around the ashes and debris with his boot. "What are you doing," Ken asked. "I have not seen any bottles. He was seen drinking yesterday," Alan said as he picked up pieces of broken glass only to discover they were from mason jars. "Who cares?" Ken said with a stress tone, "the son of bitch is dead and the world is a might greater place for it." The coroner looked up from his grim task so he could whisper to Alan, "George Kiel was loved by all I see…"

"Ken have you seen anyone other than George here Saturday night or Sunday when you were home?" Alan asked. "I don't know… what does it matter?" Ken asked, his tone becoming more agitated. Coroner Knight looked back up to Alan to see where his train of thought was leading. "The day of the murder he said he needed a drink but there was nothing in the house to drink. This morning you heard Charles Kiel state he took George here. So where did the alcohol come from?" Where are the bottles? More importantly… how the hell did a hanging man start a fire?" Alan said with a puzzled tone.

Ken stood quiet because the thought of how the fire started never crossed his mind. "Well the bottles could be anywhere in this mess," the coroner piped up, "as for the fire, maybe he started it before he hung himself. Maybe he knocked a lantern over… it was hard to tell if he snapped his neck. If he did not snap his neck, his body would flail around like a fish washed up on the beach… Last year I had a guy who hung himself off of a bridge over the railroad north of Glasford. Witnesses said he flung himself off of the bridge just in time to be hit by a train as he was hanging. When I got there his head and most of his spine was still in the noose, the rest of him was along the right of way for a quarter mile…" Ken moved away from the foundation rapidly. In the distant Alan could hear sounds of him gagging.

"Well that is all of him," Coroner Knight stated proudly as he buttoned the flap on the bag, "now how about some dinner?" Ken had returned just in time to hear the word "dinner". He quickly returned to the front yard to gag again. Alan picked up the lanterns and followed the coroner up the stone steps. Ken was leaning against a tree wiping his mouth with the back of his right hand. The coroner threw the leather bag containing George's remains into the automobile like a sack of dirty clothes.

"Please take me up to your house Mister Lynch,I could eat a horse," the coroner said with a smile. Ken looked at Coroner Knight like he himself

124

was on fire, "I'll lead ya up there, but I am not hungry. I have to… have to do something in the barn I'm sure. Alan knows his way around the house."

Alan and Coroner Knight walked up onto the porch as Ken made his way to the barn. Alan opened the screen door, "Amie? Misses Lynch?" Swiftly the voice of Amie came, "We're in the parlor Alan." The men walked in to see Amie sitting on the couch braiding Robin's hair while Grace was sitting in the rocking chair knitting a sweater. "You men ready for dinner? Where's Ken?" Grace asked as she placed the sweater in her knitting bag. "Um, he said he had things to do in the barn," Alan said. "Well we will leave some for him, you two can wash up in the kitchen. Robin and I just made a fresh batch of lye soap this morning," Grace said proudly.

The famished coroner followed Grace into the kitchen, but Alan waited for Amie. "Sorry I never returned to the restaurant for lunch. I have been running wild all day," Alan said softly to Amie. Robin got up from the floor and rolled her eyes to the young couple as she passed them. "Did you find George?" Amie asked. "Yes… just bones. Amie… he hung himself," Alan said. Amie let out a slight gasp, "I would have never thought he would do that. Drink himself to death, yes, but kill himself? It just doesn't seem possible. When will you tell his father?" Alan shrugged his shoulders, "In the morning I guess. We will drop off the bones at the funeral home tonight; I will see what the coroner

125

suggests. Amie… I'm hungry, so what's on the menu?" Amie just giggled, "Um… roast chicken…" Alan turned slightly green but food is food and he was starving.

They walked into the kitchen to see the coroner half-way through the chicken and not stopping even for a breath. "Coroner Knight, how is the chicken?" Grace asked watching the man pull apart a leg with ease. "Oh, very good ma'am! My wife doesn't cook too well. I only get a meal like this in a restaurant," the coroner said before devouring a biscuit. Amie put together a plate for her and Alan, "Come on Alan, let's eat out on the porch. It is a nice night." Alan smiled, "With pleasure. Let me know when you are ready to go back to town, coroner." The coroner grunted an acknowledgment as he shoved a spoonful of peas in his mouth.

The couple went out onto the white wooden porch and sat on the steps. The air was muggy with humidity and the smell of burned wood permeated the night. Thankfully near the house the sweet smell of the flowers Grace planted around the yard filled the air. Amie balanced the plate on her lap while Alan sat close at her side. Alan picked up a leg, took a bite then said, "This is very good. After what we just saw I did not know if I could eat for a week…" Amie looked out to the dark sky, its stars shining bright. "I wonder why he did it?" she asked. Alan stayed quiet enjoy a buttermilk biscuit. "I wonder what will happen with the farm?" Amie asked.

126

"I do not know. Since it was not his to begin with and there is no other kin to his wife, the state will take it," Alan said. Amie looked to Alan, "You know, it's not a huge farm, but the land is nice. The barn is in good shape... might make a good farm for a young couple..." Alan looked to Amie, "Do you have a couple in mind?" Amie smiled, "We could build a house right where the old one was. Dad can show you how to farm... I know you love being a law man, but you can do both if you really want..." Alan stayed quiet for a moment then said, "The best part would being coming home to you every night." Amie smiled then laid her head on Alan's shoulder.

Chapter 10

"I will be in contact with Mister Kiel this afternoon," James Heath said in his usual monotone undertaker voice, "do you have the death certificate for me to sign?" Coroner knight pulled a piece of paper out of his bag and handed it to Heath. "This states the manner of death as suicide by hanging…," Heath said with a puzzled tone. "Yes, he hung himself after he lit the house on fire," Knight said, "I looked over the remains last night in my hotel room and will file the autopsy when I return to Glasford this afternoon." Heath signed the piece of paper and handed it back to the coroner. "So much sadness has come to the Kiel family this month," Heath said with little expression. "Yes… much sadness… Good day Mister Heath," Coroner Knight said.

Waiting in his automobile, Alan sat watching the people roam about the town's stores like it was just another day. Yesterday they came together to help a friend in need, but the next day it is business as usual. "Are you ready to do this?" Alan asked the coroner as he shut the door. "You're a young buck. I have been notifying families of a loved ones death for over thirty years. It never gets easy but it's the profession I choose," the scruffy voiced man said. Alan rolled his eyes slightly as he shifted the car into gear.

The hired hands were hard at work when the men rolled up to the Kiel house to see the front door wide open allowing the morning breeze in. Alan knocked on the wooden framed screen door, its bronze screen tarnished from the humid air. It was a moment or two until they heard, "Come in! The doors' open for a reason!" Alan looked to the coroner to see his right eyebrow raised.

They walked inside to see Charles sitting at a large wooden desk. Its green leather top sat well with the dark oak frame. Charles looked up from the ledger he was writing in, "I'm guessing you found my boy…" Alan took his hat off, "Yes sir, late last night we found his body. We gave the remains to James Heath this morning. He is awaiting your word on burial plans." Charles looked back down to the ledger and wrote in a figure. Alan looked to the coroner to see him staring off into space. "Mister Kiel we found something that you may want to know," Alan said with a timid tone. Charles kept his concentration on the ledger, "Well, spit it out deputy."

Alan tried to find the words, "When we found George… um, he…" The coroner cut Alan off to speed up the announcement, "He hung himself." Charles looked up and asked, "How's that now?" Alan remained silent hoping the coroner would take over the conversation. "Well? Explain this to me?" Charles barked. "He was found in the root cellar with the support beam on top of him. Around his neck were remnants of a hemp rope,"

Alan said. Charles straightened up in his chair. He reached over to a silver floor ashtray to get his cigar and took a puff. "Deputy you tried to hang two murders on my boy. He was no murderer and I know for damn sure he would not kill himself. Now go out, do your job and find out who killed my son!" Charles said with the greatest of grief and anger. He swiveled his chair to look out the window. As the men looked on they could hear him start to weep, Alan shrugged his head toward the door as to say, "Let's get out of here."

"I will investigate this fully Mister Kiel, but I do not believe there will be any other evidence," Alan said. Charles remained facing the window and did not utter another word. The men walked out onto the porch and let the screen door slam behind them. "I'm not expected back until this afternoon. Would you like a hand looking through the rubble again?" the coroner asked. "Yes, why not. I doubt we will find anything, but we can at least try," Alan said.

July was winding down but the summer's heat was in full effect. The mid-morning sun was burning down on the two men as they sifted through the rubble. They were looking for anything that would give them a reason to think this is anything other than suicide, but with each shovelful the cemented thought of suicide was drying more. Alan would pick up every little piece of debris that looked important, but typically it was nothing of importance. The charred remains of the house looked as if they had touched the surface of the sun.

Morning slipped away and the noon hour was turning to one. The men were sitting under an elm tree relaxing in the shade. "Well I did not find one damn thing to make me think this is nothing but suicide," Alan said. The coroner wiped the sweat from his neck with a soot cover rag, "Well the counties first murder in fifteen years has been solved as far as I am concerned and the murderer saved the county the cost of rope." Alan looked over at the coroner and just shook his head. "I think I will check out the barn before we leave," Alan said. "That's fine with me," the coroner said, "I will join you in a minute, I need to relieve myself. I am guessing that is the outhouse down the hill?" Alan shook his head, "Yes, looks like a three holer..."

The red paint on the barn was faded from age and pealing from the constant abuse of the elements. Alan tugged at the sliding door, but it was stiff from the humidity. With a shrug he got the door to open enough so he could enter the structure. The smell of manure hung heavily in the air but the few animals that George owned had been removed to his father's farm. Alan looked around but nothing seemed out of place for a barn. The backroom where August slept looked as if he had just left it to work in the fields even leaving his straw bed out of sorts.

Alan walked back into the barn ready to give up the fight when he heard the floor creak oddly under his feet. He kicked the straw that covered the wood floor around to discover a trapdoor. "Did you find anything?" the coroner asked as he walked into the barn. "I don't know," Alan stated as he bent over to open the door. Alan pulled the door open to reveal a room below the barn. "Looks like a storm cellar," the coroner said," there's a lantern hanging over there, got a light?"

After lighting the lantern, Alan proceeded down a wooden ladder into the subterranean room. "Anything good down there?" Coroner Knight asked. "Yes… why don't you come down here…," Alan said with a surprised tone. Alan held the lantern up to shine a light on old wooden crates stacked to make a table or desk. On the crates were pictures of a young woman. Some of them contained a young man who looked quite familiar to Alan. "So what did you find?" came the voice from behind Alan.

Alan turned to the coroner, "A shrine I believe…" The coroner picked up one of the pictures and studied it. The picture showed a young woman sitting with a man close to her age. They looked to be in a pasture, behind them a painted mare enjoying the grass. "Is that who I think it is?" the coroner asked. "That is a very young George Kiel," Alan said, "and with him I believe to be his first wife." Alan moved the pictures around to see many of the young woman; she was very beautiful, very happy. George also looked happy, far happier than Alan had ever seen him. Alan studied the woman's face and now realized why George would stare at Amie because she holds a close resemblance to Melissa.

"He had another wife?" the coroner asked. "Yes," Alan said, "I learned about her through town gossip. Her name was Melissa. One winter they were traveling home and somehow their wagon went off the bridge. The cold water took her life. Tell me in your honest opinion; looking at the pictures does he look like an alcoholic?" The coroner looked at the pictures, "I don't know... it really hard to tell. But what I do see is a man who looked very happy, very much in love... What year did she die?" Alan thought for a second, "Eighty-nine I believe."

"Funny I do not remember that," the coroner said. "Well from what I was told her family was not happy and they asked for a murder investigation. They never got it, but Charles Kiel did buy their farm from them." The coroner smirked, "Sounds like they were rewarded to keep their mouth closed." Alan looked at him with an inquisitive expression, "I think it is time to stop listening to town gossip and look closer at the Kiel family. Help me collect these photos and anything else."

Alan parked the automobile at the interurban platform. "I will tell Lange everything that has transpired. I am sure he will think the murder investigation is over, but that is truly up to you deputy," Coroner Knight said as he stepped onto the platform. "I just want to make sure everyone gets the respect they deserve in death as they should have gotten in life," Alan said, "I think I will start by looking up the death of his original wife. There must be some kind of file that will give me better information than the memories of a bunch of old men."

The interurban streetcar slowed down to a stop in front of the platform where the two men are talking. "Deputy I believe there may be a change in plans...," the coroner said as he nodded toward the train. Stepping onto the platform was a talk, husky man wearing a brown suit. Hanging below the bottom of his jacket was the gold chain of a pocket watch that matched well to the shiny brass badge he wore on his jacket. "Deputy Johnson, Coroner Knight," the man said with a deep, ballsy voice.

"Sheriff Bonner, Sir," Alan said with respect. "So nice to see both of you working so well together...," the sheriff said bluntly. "Nice seeing you again Jimmy," the coroner said, "but I need to get back to town. Come call on me sometime, we can go bowl a frame or two." Alan watched as the two old friends shook hands before the Coroner stepped onto the streetcar in time for it to leave.

"Deputy, let's go back to your office. We need to talk," the sheriff said. "Yes Sir," Alan said feeling like a child about to be scolded. "Deputy we do not need to be so formal, please call me James and I will call you Alan," the slightly jolly man said. "Yes… James," Alan said with a guarded tone.

The men walked into the small office that Alan held in town. Alan sat in his worn wooden chair while the sheriff remained standing looking over the office. "Alan you are a great deputy. You were the top in your class and you come from a family of officers. However I have received many calls about you," James said. "May I guess the calls are coming from Charles Kiel?" Alan asked. The Sheriff sat down facing Alan. "I would not be lying if I said that certain people wield more power than others. The Kiel family, specifically Charles, has far more power," James said with the tone of a father talking to his young son, "I have heard about what happened and that George Kiel is now dead. It is assumed that the murderer is now dead and the investigation should stop. I am not telling you to do that… but I am telling you to do your job and if you feel you need to follow leads in an unofficial role… so be it."

Alan leaned back in his chair, "Sir… James, are you saying that I can keep the investigation going?" James rubbed his goatee than said, "From what I have heard, there was much more to the murders than it looks like on the surface. Even if the suspected murderer is now dead, that does not mean the investigation should stop. I just want you to step lightly around the Kiel family. Their power can cause careers to be lost. Do you understand Alan?" The young deputy stayed quiet for a minute waiting for further fatherly advice. "Alan, you looked surprised," James said with a blank expression.

Alan cleared his throat, "I will be honest, I thought you were going to tell me to drop the investigation altogether and keep away from Charles Kiel." The sheriff laughed heartily then said in a reassuring tone, "You have no reason to think I would ever cave to anyone with money. Alan… you have the luxury of being both a police officer and a detective. You have the smallest town to patrol but also the largest area of farm land. You have to admit your job is not that difficult and I started in an office just like this. I know how boring going after chicken thieves and breaking up bar fights can be. This is your investigation, do what you feel you need to do, but do it correctly and tread lightly."

Alan pulled out the photographs of Melissa Kiel that were found in the storm shelter and laid them in front of the sheriff. "I found these this morning in a storm shelter under George's barn. It was almost a shrine to his first wife. I want to include her death in my investigation," Alan said. The sheriff picked up one of the photographs. It showed a beautiful young woman, her hair braided and laying down her left side. "Was he suspected of murdering her also?" the sheriff asked. "From what I have been told it was an accident, but Coroner Knight made a queer statement this morning. He said he does not remember her dying. That man

136

may be odd at times, but he has a memory like an elephant. I was going to talk with the town recorder in the morning to see what information I can find about her. I do not even know where she is buried. I heard her parents moved to Galena. I thought I may call on them," Alan said.

The clock on the wall chimed to announce it was four o'clock. "I better be getting back to Glasford," James said, "Let the evidence take you where you need to go. If you do need to travel to Galena, make sure you get an officer to watch your post while you are gone." Alan stood to walk the sheriff back to the streetcar platform. "I will keep you informed, sir," Alan said as he escorted the man out of the office. "Just make sure you are careful who you speak to about the investigation…," James said with a mildly stern tone. Alan took what the sheriff was saying as not just advice, but an order, "Yes Sheriff Bonner."

The streets of the small town were quieting down for the early evening. As the sheriff and his deputy walked to the streetcar line, they could feel the eyes of the townspeople on them. "Alan, do you ever get the feeling you are being watched from all directions?" the sheriff asked with a humorous tone. "Uh, huh… all the time and it has gotten worse in the past few weeks," Alan said with all seriousness.

Chapter 11

A few days has passed since Sheriff Bonner paid a visit to Alan. The investigation took a back seat to the very examples the sheriff gave of boring police work. During the days the heat was squelched by driving rains that kept the men out of the fields and in the town's tavern. This kept Alan's hands full of fighting and drunkenness, but now the sun has returned and so has the field work. With justice returned to Mill Grove, Alan can go back to the investigation.

Sitting in the backroom of the office are three wooden filing cabinets containing the files of all police matters dealing with Mill Grove. The files were far from complete, organization was never followed and spelling was an art not yet discovered by Alan's predecessors. With every drawer Alan opened, more of a mess piled out onto the floor. Coffee covered papers, cigar butts and mouse excrement were the main items found.

Alan spent the good part of the day trying to organize the paperwork so he could search for anything that would tell him about the accident that killed Melissa Kiel. When all the papers were looked at and placed back into the filing cabinet in some form of order, Alan knew nothing more about the death of Melissa Kiel than idle gossip of old men.

Never one to give up without a fight, Alan decided the next stop would be the town hall. Alan walked down the steps of the town hall and made sure to bypass the mayor's office as quickly as he could. He managed to stay away from the mayor since the night of the dance and he wanted to keep his luck going.

The recorder of deeds took care of all records for Mill Grove and Prairie Township. Charged with this duty is Gordon Higgins. He had been charged with the job decades before and continues on simply because no else wants to do it. Alan walked in to find the elderly man asleep at his desk with the day's newspaper in his hands and pot of coffee boiling dry on a hot plate.

"Gordon!" Alan shouted. The man continued to snore; his hearing was not the best since he was injured at the Battle of Hartville. "Gordon! Your hot plate just burned the building down!" Alan shouted three feet from the man's good ear. The response was the same so Alan walked over and turned the hot plate off. "Son of a bitch!" Alan yelled as he was shocked turning the knob. "What was that? Who's there?" Gordon demanded as he woke up.

"Gordon, its Alan Johnson" The recorder searched around for his glasses to see who was talking to him. "They're on you head Gordon," Alan said trying not to laugh. Gordon reached up and pulled his wire rimmed glasses down to bring Alan into focus. "Alan… good to see you again. How can I help you?" Gordon asked. Alan sat on a wooden stool in front of the recorders desk. "Gordon, I need to find a marriage license and a death certificate," Alan said. "I am guessing that the person will be on both?" Gordon asked with a curious tone. "Yes. Melissa Kiel," Alan said.

Gordon cleared his throat and pretended that he did not hear the name, "Who's that again?" Alan leaned forward, "Melissa Kiel!" Gordon took his glasses off and wiped the sleep out of his eyes. "She died years ago… sometime in the eighties," Gordon said in a somber tone. "Yes, eighty-nine during the winter. They were married a few years prior. Can I see the documents please?" Alan asked with a forceful tone as his patience was wearing thin rapidly.

The elderly man took to his feet with a groan and shuffled over to a bank of filing cabinets. "I'll get the marriage certificate first, let me look in this book here for the date," Gordon said as he pulled a thick red leather bound book of off one of the cabinets. He opened it and looked for the letter K. After a few pages he said, "April of eighty-six." He opened the cabinet below and looked through the papers. "Here you go deputy, the marriage certificate," Gordon said as he handed the paper to Alan, "I will look for her death certificate next." Alan looked at the marriage certificate to finally see Melissa's maiden name, Pugh.

"Her last name was Pugh," Alan said out loud. "Yes, I could have told you that deputy," Gordon said as he was looking through another book of records, "I cannot find an entry for her death." Alan placed the marriage certificate on the desk, "What do you mean you cannot find an entry for her death?" Gordon turned around and sat down at his chair, "It is not entered in the book. My memory is not the best, but I do not remember a death certificate being entered."

Alan sat back in the chair, "Do you remember what happened?" Gordon closed the book carefully and looked at Alan, "I believe she fell in the river and died from the cold. They were young, so young. You know how those young couples were, always in love…" Alan looked to Gordon puzzled, "I thought he was mean to her, always drinking?" Gordon shook his head, "No, no. Not as I remember. He was never the most intelligent man, but he loved that girl."

"Do you remember where she was buried?" Alan asked. "Somewhere out west, far west I believe. Outside the county," Gordon said looking to wall as if it would revive his memory. "Galena?" Alan asked. "Yes… I believe that was it," Gordon said with a reassured tone.

"Do you remember her family trying to have a murder investigation opened against George?" Alan asked. Gordon took his glasses off once again to rub his eyes. He placed the glasses back on and tried to focus his eyes on Alan. "No I do not remember that. I do believe her family moved not long after… to Galena I think was. I actually think Charles Kiel bought their farm… I should have the deed," Gordon said then yawned.

"No, I have taken enough of your time up Gordon… Say, what were her parents' names?" Alan asked as he stood up. Gordon scratched his head and searched his mind for the names, "Cliff… Clifton and Ellie if I remember correctly. They were older, had their daughter late in life. Nice people. They left without saying goodbye to many people. Guess losing a daughter makes you forget about friends and neighbors." Alan pulled a notepad out of his breast pocket and wrote the names down. "What does all of this have to do with the murders?" Gordon asked. "I do not know, just a feeling I have," Alan said, "Hey, where was their farm?"

Gordon looked up to a township map mounted on the wall behind his desk, "There, on Beldon road just off of the Illinois Central tracks. They had a nice farm… had the first poured cement silo in the township. Come to think about it, he put that silo in the summer before his daughter died…" Alan looked at the map, "I know that area. There is a path that leads into the field… to a concrete silo…"

"After Charles took title of the property I think he had the barn and house removed. Had no

142

need for them I guess… couldn't take that silo though. Guess that was Cliff's mark on the land," Gordon said with a chuckle. "Well, thank you for the help Gordon," Alan said as he moved toward the door to leave, "Hey Gordon, how did Charles remove the house and barn?" Gordon looked off to the side in thought and then back to Alan, "The house burned down I believe. Can't remember what happened to the barn. I guess he had it burned also."

Beldon road curved to take a path north by west just outside of Mill Grove and went as far as Hazelton. Charles Kiel's farm backed up to Beldon road where the Illinois Central railroad tracks bisected the road. On the opposite is a pasture that is used for grazing of cattle and lambs. On the property past an iron cattle gate was a gravel path that leads toward an old concrete silo just off of the tracks. The silo's steel domed roof was rusted and partially missing.

Alan rolled carefully over the railroad tracks then parked at the side of the road in front of the cattle gate. The gate was locked with a pad lock but that would not keep Alan from climbing over the gate. He followed the path into the meadow past a group of grazing cows whose moos announced Alan's presence. Alan followed the path to an area that resembled a farm; old pieces of glass and rusting pieces of steel were seen under the deep brush. The ground was very uneven in spots and it became quickly apparent that a house had been there. Kicking over the tall strands of grass exposed the edges of the old stone foundation.

Just to the east of the house an iron well pump came out of the ground and stood just above the grasses. Its handle was long gone as was the wooden planks that used to cover the well shaft. It is at this moment Alan noticed a trail heading through the weeds toward the silo. Alan followed the path through deep brush, burr bushes and clumps of ragweed. As he followed the path to the side of the silo he saw it followed the circumference to its south side. This side of the silo was only about ten feet from the railroad tracks.

What Alan discovered puzzled him. From the weeds and scrub bushes that surround most of the silo, this side was covered with rose bushes; red roses, yellow roses and some pink. At the base of the silo was a small wooden cross, on its face letters were carved. "Melissa," Alan said with a somber tone. Alan knelt down and pulled away some stray weeds that were trying to obscure the cross. Just as he pulled the weeds away, he heard footsteps behind him.

"I heard some of the old fools of this town were tells tales, but I didn't suspect you would listen to them deputy," Charles said. Alan stood up and turned to see the elderly man dressed in bib overalls and a faded flannel shirt. "I never heard the story before," Alan said, "I do not know what to believe any longer." Charles walked past Alan and smelled one of the yellow roses. "When she died her parents wanted her buried on their farm. George objected, but finally gave in to them. That spring he and her father dug her grave. The tracks were not here then. Her father said a horse she had as a girl is buried here and they wanted them to be together again."

Alan looked to the roses and asked, "I guess he still came here after all these years?" Charles sat down on a tree stump and said, "Yes… Rebecca did not know all about Melissa. She did not know this is where he went when life got too stressful for him. I came here many times looking for him… only to find him sitting next to the cross. You never forget about the first woman you fall in love with and George thought about her always." Alan listen to Charles speak in a tone that expressed sadness and understanding. "They said it was an accident. The wagon slipped off of the bridge and she landed in the water," Alan said.

Charles looked off toward the tracks as the sound of an approaching train came from a distance. "He almost broke down our door as he pushed it in, carrying her limp body in his arms. Her skin… her skin was turning blue and her coat, her dress had ice formed on them. He took her to the fireplace and held her tight in front of the fire. One my other boys brought the doctor but it was too late. The life was already draining from her tiny body. That night my boy died along with her. He was nothing but a shell of a man since then," Charles said. As he ended his last sentence an Illinois Central passenger train rocketed past the men; its huge driving wheels made Alan look tiny, the wind they generated knocked the flowers about. As Alan watched the train pass, he tried not to notice Charles sitting on the stump crying.

Once the last car passed Alan stepped to the sad man, "Come on, I'll walked you back out to the road." Charles stood with a moan and a creak of his joints. Alan worked up the courage to ask Charles one last question, "Was it true that Melissa's parents did not believe that the accident happened as he said?" Charles stopped, picked a rose and held it in his hand as he started to walk again. "No, they were sad as you would expect any parent would be. The gossips had turned this into something more than it was. George never drank a drop of alcohol until long after Melissa's passing. Her parents were older; they did not have the strength to farm any longer. I offered to buy the farm and give it to George so he could be with his Melissa. Right after they moved out west there was a terrific storm, lightning must have struck the house and burned it down. I told George we would rebuild it, but he did not want to. I do not know why, just did not want to do it."

The men came to the road where Alan's REO was parked alone on the side. "How did you get out here?" Alan asked. "I walk my land daily, boy. I also come by to say hello to that young girl often. I did not know you would be trespassing on my land. Just happened upon you," Charles said. "Why don't you get in the car and I will take you back to your house," Alan said.

As they took off down the road, Charles looked to Alan, "Deputy, I was not lying when I said my boy would have never taken his life. He has been through a lot and down many dark paths, but he would never take his life… never." Alan slowed down to turn onto Spring Valley road, being careful to creep past the towering stalks of corn. As he made the turn he asked, "What about Rebecca and her mother?" Charles cleared his throat, "I do not think he could have done that either. I am not speaking as a father right now, but of a man who has seen a lot in his life. He did not murder those women. I do not know what exactly happened, but I do know he did not do it!"

Alan turned into the driveway of Charles' farm but stopped the car under an oak tree way before getting to the house. Alan put the automobile in park, but left it engine running. "Why did he marry Rebecca?" Alan asked bluntly. "I thought he needed a woman to repair his soul and put the spirit back into him. However it just made his life more complicated. One day he came to me and told me that he was injured in that accident. An injury he did not know that was inflicted on him until long after the accident. Because of it he was not able to be a father and that was the final blow to his soul. Rebecca was a good woman, but for George, she

147

was not Melissa and that is who he wanted. I hope God had mercy on my boy and he is with Melissa again," Charles said with a trembled voice, "promise you will find who killed him. None of us know how much time we have; I hope I have enough to see my boys' name cleared." Alan chose his words carefully as he slipped the car into first gear with a slight jerk, "Sir, I will do my best."

After delivering Charles to his front porch, Alan left swiftly and turned toward the Lynch farm. He slowed down just in time to see Amie helping her mother remove clothes from the clothesline in the side yard. He got out of the car before it completely stopped then walked straight to Amie. "Alan," Amie said with surprise. Alan did not say a word as he wrapped his arms around her body, pulled her close and kissed her on the lips. Amie offered no resistance and almost went limp in his arms while her mother watched in awe. Alan slowly pulled back from her lips and said with deep sincerity, "Amie I hope you know how much I love you and know I will always love you."

Chapter 12

It was well past eleven o'clock when Alan decided to turn in for the night. He was just topping his stairs when a knock came at his front door. Alan reluctantly went back down the stairs and turned on the porch light as he was unlocking the door. He opened the door to find a woman who looked to be in her forties; her skin wrinkled, her black hair stained with streaks of silver. Alan immediately noticed her lip was swollen and a small pool of dried blood in the left corner of her mouth.

"Deputy Johnson?" the woman asked. "Yes, please come in. What happened?" Alan asked as the women walked in carrying a leather suitcase. "You do not know me, I'm Oliva Kiel." the woman said with a raspy voice. "Please some sit down," Alan said as he turned on the parlor light and gestured to a wingback chair.

"I do not have much time deputy. I want to be on the midnight streetcar to Glasford," Olivia said. "Who did this?" Alan asked. "My husband Phillip… and it will be the last time. Our children are grown and on their own. I took his abuse for over twenty years; it's time to move on!" Olivia said with a raised tone. "Well what can I do for you?" Alan asked.

"I have no proof, but I believe Philip is the one you are looking for," Olivia said with a smug tone. "Looking for?" Alan asked. "For the murders! I think he killed Becky and her mother. I also think he killed George," Olivia said with a very smug tone. "Why do you think this?" Alan asked drinking the information in.

"Philip has a real vendetta against his father. He always had. He's the oldest and while George was handled lightly by their father, Philip was never good enough for Charles. I found out he has been buying land up around his father's farm. One of the last pieces he needed was Martha's," Olivia said as if she was running from the devil. "But you have no real proof he did anything wrong…," Alan said fishing for more information.

"No I have no proof, but you now have more information than you did before, don't you?" Olivia said with bluntness. "Yes I believe I do… Where will you go once you get to Glasford?" Alan asked feeling put in his place. "My mother lives in Chicago so I will take the train there. I never want to see this one horse town again. Philip can see what it is like to not have a woman take care of his every need and desire," Olivia said with renewed anger, "our cook will make his meals, but she does not have what he wants… anytime of the day…"

"Um… may I ask what happened this evening?" Alan asked trying to avoid hearing too much information. "It was a typical night. He came home drunk and thought I was sleeping with one of the farm hands. He is a violent man. When our daughters were old enough, they married off so they could get out of the house. I told him to sleep it off in one of the other rooms so he hit me… like he does every night," Olivia said with a softened tone.

"He will come after you," Alan said with compassion. "Let him, my brother is a detective for the Chicago police. I am sure he will take care of Philip. But hopefully you will get him in a jail cell before anything happens to me," Olivia said then looked to the mantle clock to see it was ten minutes to midnight, "I better get going deputy. Please get him; he does not deserve to get away with murder."

Alan walked the woman to the door, "Perhaps I should walk you to the streetcar," Alan said. "No, I will be fine. When I left he was passed out in his rocking chair. He probably will not wake until morning," Olivia said as she walked out onto the porch. "Misses Kiel, if I need to contact you, where can I do so?" Alan asked. "My mother lives at one-eighteen Polk Street, but please only contact me if I truly need to. Good night," Olivia said. Alan watched the woman walk down the deserted sidewalk lit by the occasional light of a passing house or business. When she was out of sight, he closed the door and turned off the lights.

Once Alan was allowed to fall asleep, the morning greeted him rapidly. He had a pot of coffee along with a shock from the hot plate to get his system going. He made his rounds but could not forget what Olivia Kiel had told him. He decided investigating this new information should be his top priority.

Gordon walked into his office to find Alan sitting in his chair waiting for him. "Deputy?" Gordon asked as he passed through the doorframe. "Good morning or should I say good afternoon, Gordon. I need to look at your plat books," Alan said bluntly. Gordon scratched his head then asked, "Where do you need to look at?" Alan stood up from the chair, "All properties around Charles Kiel's estate." Gordon looked away a moment then back to Alan, "North-east quarter for section sixty-three." Alan looked at Gordon and shook his head in disbelief.

Gordon pulled out a large plat book and placed it down on his desk, almost losing his grip do to its weight. He opened the book looking for section sixty-three. "Here you go deputy," Gordon said as he pointed out Charles' property. Alan looked at the property then the ones surrounding it. Many of the properties had the same name, Philip Kiel. "Wait a minute, this is the Brown farm on Spring Valley road but it states Philip Kiel," Alan said. Gordon looked at the book, "That is correct. Philip bought their mortgage from the bank. It's all perfectly legal and as long as they continue to make their payments, they still legally own the property," Gordon said.

Alan looked to Gordon, "If they do not make their payments?" Gordon shrugged his shoulders, "They would be foreclosed on." Alan looked back to the book to see the Vogal farm and across the road from it was another parcel with the name of Philip Kiel. "This book cannot be correct Gordon. Look here, this parcel is marked for Philip Kiel, but that is Kenneth Lynch's property," Alan said. Gordon reached into a wooden file holder and pulled out a piece of paper, "Philip Kiel bought the mortgage from the Farmers Bank last year. Kenneth just filed this paperwork last week. He paid the mortgage off and is now the sole owner of the property." Alan took the paper from Gordon and looked to see the signatures of both Philip and Ken on the form. Also marked was the payoff amount of one hundred dollars.

"Can you pull the paperwork for when Philip originally bought this property?" Alan asked. Gordon shook his head in agreement and walked over to one of many filing cabinets. "This is it," Gordon said as he handed the paperwork over. Alan looked at it to see Philip bought the property from the Farmers bank for the sum of six thousand, seven hundred, and fifty-five dollars. Alan did not say a word but just handed the papers back to Gordon. "Thank you for the help Gordon," Alan said as he walked out of the office.

Alan walked out onto the street from the town hall. He was quickly making his way to his office when he heard someone calling his name.

153

Alan turned to see August Palmer standing behind him. "Deputy, I just heard the news about George. Is it true he killed himself?" August asked. "I really do not have time to speak about it right now August. Come back some other time," Alan said in a rushed tone. "Deputy… Alan, please I want to know what is going on," August asked with sincerely.

Alan stopped dead in his tracks and turned back to August. "How much time do you have right now?" Alan asked in haste. "I'm waiting on them to unload the wagon at the grain mill, I don't know, half hour or so?" August said in a skeptical tone. "Good, come with me," Alan said as he took off in a rapid pace again. August could barely keep up with Alan as the pace he took only accelerated toward his office.

The glass rattled as Alan let the door slam wide open as he went into the office and proceeded to a closet door. He removed a skeleton key from his belt to unlock the door. "August I need your help," Alan said as he removed a revolver from the closet, "This is the gun from the murders. I want you to help me with an experiment." August stood slightly dumfounded by what he was witnessing. "What do I need to do?" August asked. Alan opened the chamber and loaded it with bullets, "We're going out to the farm, come on."

As the men drove out to the farm, the gun sat on Alan's lap, its muzzle pointing uncomfortably at August. "Hey Alan, can you turn that gun around and point it toward your door? I'm afraid one of these bumps might set it off," August said bluntly. "Don't worry, we are almost there," Alan said as he swerved to miss the bumps and runts in the dirt road.

As to his word, they quickly arrived at the burned out homestead. Alan handed the gun to August, "I want you to go over near the foundation and stand right where the kitchen porch was." August took the gun and looked down at it, "What do you want me to do?" Alan looked up to the Lynch farmhouse, "I will be on the porch with Kenneth. When I wave my hand I want you to fire a shot out into the cornfield. You will fire four shots total but only do it when I gesture toward you, understand?" August shook his head slowly in agreement and stepped out of the automobile.

Before August could close the door, Alan took up the driveway to the Lynch farm. As he stopped at the house he saw Robin feeding the chickens in a pen off of the barn. "Where is your father?" Alan asked the young woman. "In the barn… why are you in such a rush for?" Robin asked. Before Alan could respond Kenneth came out of the barn hearing the conversation. "Deputy, what are you doing here?" Kenneth asked. "We need to talk… alone," Alan said sternly. Kenneth looked at Robin, "You have more chores to do, go get to them as the deputy and I have a conversation."

"Let's go to the front porch," Alan stated then turned toward the front of the house. Kenneth reluctantly followed. "What is this all about Alan?" Kenneth asked in an angered tone. "On the day of the murders you said you were sitting in that chair next to the front door," Alan said. "Yes, like I have told you countless times," Ken said as his anger started to grow. "You also said you did not hear any of the shots and did not know that anything had happened until George ran up the hill asking for help," Alan said as he pulled the chair away from the door and placed it at Ken's feet. "Yes for Christ's sake. What the hell is all of this about?" Kenneth asked.

Alan pointed to the chair and said forcefully, "Please put the chair right where you had it and sit down." Ken looked at Alan, but knowing the daylight was slipping away decided to humor him. Ken picked the chair up and placed it near the door. "Okay, now what do you need to know?" Ken asked as he sat down. Alan looked over to the Vogal farm to see August waiting. Alan lifted his hand in the air, and then swiftly arced it down to his side. August saw the sign, pointed the pistol toward the cornfield and pulled the trigger.

Alan could hear a pop that echoed between the barns, the house and the surrounding fields. Ken quickly winced at the sound, and then closed his eyes as if to say to Alan, "Now I understand why I am here." Alan looked to Ken, "What did you just hear?" Ken opened his eyes, "It sounded like a shot,

156

I guess, it's hard to tell." Alan looked back to August and again waved his hand down. August aimed then fired the pistol. "There it is again. You know that sounds like gunfire to me," Alan said bluntly to Kenneth who was now red in the face with anger.

"What are you trying to prove Deputy?" Ken asked while trying to hold back his boiling anger. "I'm proving that you did hear the shots that morning and I want to know why you lied to me about it," Alan said with anger. Ken stood up and placed himself directly in front of Alan, "I have nothing to say to you. Get the hell off of my property and stay away from my daughter while you're at it. The only man I will allow to marry her is someone who was born in the country and knows country ways, not a city boy protected by a tin badge. Now go!"

Alan stood his ground in front of Kenneth, "I did some digging. It appears Philip Kiel held the note on your property. He just bought it last year for over six thousand dollars, but you managed to pay all of that off in a year. I don't believe it. I think Philip gave you the title so you would keep your mouth shut." Ken clinched his teeth, "Boy you are on dangerous ground right now. Do not dare try to tell me what you think I have or have not done. I told you once to get off my property. I am not going to do it again."

The tension between the two men was broke by the slam of the screen door. "What are you two yelling about?" Grace asked as she dried her hands on her apron. "Nothing. The deputy here is about to walk to his motorize buggy and leave," Ken said while staring Alan down. Alan did not move, not even to swat away a fly that kept landing on his forehead. "One of you tell me what is going on," Grace demanded. "Let me demonstrate," Alan said as he flagged August. Instantly another shot reverberated through the barnyard. "What was that?" Grace asked as she looked toward the Vogal farm.

"That was gunfire. I asked August Palmer to fire a shot whenever I waved to him. You see, your husband stated he did not hear any shots the day of the murders, yet as you just heard, that cannot be," Alan said with a smug tone. "Kenneth, is that true?" Grace asked of her steaming husband. Without saying a word, Kenneth left the porch and steamed off toward the machine shed.

"What is going on?" Grace asked Alan. "I believe your husband should tell you, it is not my place," Alan said. "That is what he is going to do, follow me," Grace said as she took off after her husband. They entered the machine shed to see Kenneth sitting on a stool next to an upturned plow. His face was contorted with anger as he ran a file down the blade to sharpen it. "What the hell are you still doing here?" Kenneth asked when he noticed Alan.

"You are going to tell me why you are so angry!" Grace said with a stern, motherly tone. Kenneth took another pass down the plow and then felt the edge with his right thumb. "The deputy here thinks I have more knowledge about the murders than I have told him," Kenneth said as he looked down the profile of the plow. "If you know something, tell Alan right now!" Grace said loud enough to cause Alan to jump a bit. Kenneth threw the file down on the workbench, "Don't be telling me what to do woman. I make the decisions around here and I made one… I made the right decision!"

Grace looked over to Alan and then back to Kenneth, "What are you talking about?" Alan felt the atmosphere becoming very uncomfortable. Kenneth leaned back against the workbench and wiped his hands with a dirty rag, "George was shot and he did run to me for help. Right before you arrived at Charles' place, Philip Kiel arrived on horseback, but from the other direction. It was as if he knew what happened. He pulled me aside and told me that if I said what he wanted, I would have my farm clear and free." Grace's mouth dropped at Kenneth's revelation, "Ken? What is wrong with you? You lied to the police!" Alan saw that Kenneth was very remorseful of his acts.

"Did you see Philip at the house?" Alan asked. "No… I am truthful with that, I did not see anything," Kenneth said. "I never saw Philip when I arrived at Charles Kiel's farm and August never said he saw him," Alan said. "He was out in the barn. I went outside to smoke while waiting for you and the doctor when he rode up. I do not think Charles even knew he was there."

"Did George tell you what happened?" Alan asked. Kenneth shook his head, "No he said Rebecca did it." Alan rubbed his chin, "Why did he say Rebecca shot him and then told August the same fib?" Kenneth shrugged his shoulders, "That was his story. I am sure he was afraid of Philip. Maybe that is why he said Rebecca did it. All I know is that Philip wanted me to say what George told me... and say I did not hear the shots. I thought I would not be lying because that is what I know. Yes I heard the shots... but I figured George pulled the trigger." Alan looked out the doorway toward the Vogal farm, "You said Philip was on horseback. Did you see his horse over there?" Ken shook his head, "No."

Grace wiped a tear from her left eye, "Why did you not just tell the truth, Ken?" Kenneth threw the rag on the floor and picked up the file, "Look around! We have worked our hands to the bone and we still owed our souls to the bank. He said all I had to do was say that George said it was Rebecca and that he would make the bank forgive our mortgage. Why would I not do that?" Grace looked to Alan, "Look at the man I married! I never thought he would ever do anything like this, but he always surprises me in some way. I never thought he would lie to protect a murderer!"

"There is more to Philip than I think you know… He has been buying up the notes on all of the farms in the area. He was going to take all of your properties over just so he could out do his father I believe," Alan said. "Why did he kill Rebecca and Martha?" Grace asked. "Martha was going to lease her farm to August's brother. I think he tried to get the property and I am sure she said no," Alan said, "Ken, I need you to talk to the state's attorney." Kenneth's face turned red, "No! I cannot risk my farm… my family. He killed two innocent women, think of what he could do to my family!"

"Ken you need to make this right. I know you were never fond of George, but if you can prove he was innocent, it will let his soul rest in peace," Grace said. "Philip Kiel is not of a right mind. I have you and the girls to worry about," Kenneth said bluntly. "Ken… I cannot tell you everything will be alright, but this is the right thing to do," Alan said sincerely. "The right thing to do? Who are you to tell me what is right and wrong?" Kenneth asked with a renewed anger, "You live in a black and white world, but the rest of us live in shades of gray. I am not going to put the lives of my family at risk so I can clear the name of a dead man!"

Graced walked out of the door and turned back toward Kenneth, "You have changed with age Ken. I remember a time when you would fight the devil himself and do it for anyone in need. You have

161

to set this right and you need to do it now!"
Kenneth watched as his wife walked away in a huff.
"You know all I have is a story. I have no evidence,"
Kenneth said with a blank expression. "It's a start,"
Alan said.

Chapter 13

"All you have are stories and no evidence!" Lange yelled at Alan. Kenneth was sitting next to him and felt just as small as Alan did at that moment. "I know there is little evidence, but I think there is enough to the stories to allow me to interview Philip Kiel," Alan said with a strong, persuasive tone. Lange sat behind his carved maple desk fuming, "Deputy, as far as I am concerned the murderer killed himself and there is no reason to look further into this matter. Take my advice, forget about these people and move on while you still have a job!"

Kenneth stood up to walk out of the office, "I knew this was a waste of time deputy. When you have a blowhard politician deciding what is and is not worthy of prosecution, there will never be any justice for those women. I need to get back to the farm; I have real work to do." Lange could not believe what the farmer had just said in his presence and Alan was feeling the need to flee. "A dirt farmer has the gall to call me a blowhard? Get the hell out of my office... both of you!" Lange's bellow was loud enough to echo down the halls.

Alan stood, placed his hat on his head and said, "I think being called a politician is far worse than being called a blowhard..." Lange was doing a slow burn as the men walked out of his office with the slam of the door. "There, I did as you asked and went to see the states attorney. For this nothing was done and I am out an afternoon's worth of work," Kenneth said as he rolled a cigarette. "I cannot believe that man. He wanted to string-up George with no evidence but he will not allow me to talk to Phillip," Alan said as they walked through the lobby of the brick building, "I think we have just found that Charles Kiel is no longer the most powerful man in the county, it is now his son Philip. Let's get down to the streetcar station and go home." As they walked out of the county building they passed a poster on an easel showing Lange's picture and his platform for reelection. At the bottom was his slogan, "Justice for all, worries for none."

     As with most afternoons, the restaurant was quiet without customers allowing Amie to sit on a stool behind the lunch counter reading a magazine. She was slowly turning the pages of the magazine showing the modern fashions of New York and Paris, when the door of the restaurant opened startling her. A man walked in, his clothes as dirty as his skin. He went to the counter and sat down. "Got any coffee?" the man asked with a gravely tone. "Yes sir," Amie replied as she reached under the counter for a cup. She placed the cup before the man and turned to get the coffee pot off of the stove.

     "Keep looking that way little lady and you won't get hurt…," the man said as she heard the sound of a gun cocking. "Mister I don't have much money but you can have all of it," Amie said softly. The man walked around the counter and placed his arms around her waist. She could feel the cold steel of a revolver in his left hand. "I have a message for your father and your man... Tell them to mind their business and all will be well," the man whispered into Amie's ear. He moved his right hand over her clothes up her stomach then over her right breast, "If they do not, I will be back to visit both you and your sister. Do you understand?" Amie shook her head in agreement as tears started to flow down her cheeks.

"Now keep facing that stove until I leave the restaurant," the man said as he slowly removed his hands from Amie's body. He placed the gun back into his pants pocket and backed out of the restaurant. Amie did as she was told until she heard the door close. She turned around and looked toward the windows to hopefully catch another glimpse of the man. She ran to the door, opened it and walked out onto the sidewalk, but the man had disappeared. A group of women were coming toward Amie. "Excuse me, did you just see a man leave the restaurant?" Amie asked with slight panic. The women looked at one another. "No," one of them said, "sorry."

Amie left the women and ran over to Alan's office only to find the door locked. She went to walk back to the restaurant when she heard the screech of the streetcar coming to a stop. She looked down the street to see two men stepping off onto the wooden platform. "That looks like dad and Alan," Amie said out loud. She walked down the sidewalk toward the men to see it was indeed her father and her boyfriend. As they grew closer Amie increased her speed until she was almost at a full run.

"Amie, what's wrong?" Alan asked as she wrapped her arms around him and started to cry. "There was a man. I thought he was going to rob me but… but it was much worse," Amie said between bouts of tears. "What happened?" Kenneth demanded. "He told me to tell both of you to mind your own businesses or else…," Amie said, her voice cracking. "Or else what?" Alan asked as he wrapped his arms around the shaking woman. "He would come visit me and Robin… he then… he…," Amie said softly so others on the sidewalk would not hear. Kenneth's face had turned beat red, "What did he do?" Amie rested her head on Alan's chest, "He touched me, my breasts…" Alan's grip grew tighter as his anger escalated.

"Let's go back to the restaurant," Alan said, "I want you to describe him as much as you can." They walked into the restaurant and sat around one of the tables. "What did he look like?" Kenneth asked before Alan could open his mouth. "He was dirty, very dirty. His clothes, his skin… he smelled bad," Amie said. "What did he wear, was he short, tall?" Alan asked. "Um I do not know his height… his breath hit the top of my head. He was thin and

166

he had a thin mustache, black hair and brown eyes I think. I really did not see his eyes that good," Amie said as she started to cry again, "I do not remember much else. I think he had jeans but I cannot remember what type of shirt or color." Alan took Amie's hand, "Its fine honey. I will find him, trust me."

"He better pray you find him before I do," Kenneth said under his breath. "Why don't you take Amie home and stay there with your family. I will go find this man… alone," Alan said firmly to Kenneth. "I can take care of my girl's deputy. You know, I told you I wanted to have nothing to do with this and look at what happened!" Kenneth said as his anger started to unleash. Alan looked to Amie, then to Kenneth, "No one knew that you were going with me to Glasford. No one had knowledge of what you knew except Grace and me. No one until…" Kenneth's eyes grew wide, "Lange."

Amie looked at both of the men, "What were you two doing together? What were you on the streetcar for?" Alan looked to Kenneth and then back to Amie, "Your father will fill you in on your way back to the farm. Ken, you two better get moving. I have someone I need to call on."

Kenneth clenched his teeth, "Come on Amie. Your mother should have dinner on soon." Alan stood to help Amie up from her chair like a good gentleman when Amie heard Alan's boots on the wood floor. "Alan, he had boots on. I remember the sound of boots on the wood floor," Amie said. "Good, that will help," Alan said then kissed her on the lips. "Ken, take care of your family. I will be by to talk to you later this evening."

Alan left the restaurant, crossed the street and entered the doorway to the telephone exchange. He climbed the stairs to find Sarah sitting at her exchange listening in on juicy gossip. Alan cleaned his throat then said softly, "Ah, Sarah?" The operator looked up in surprise and almost threw the headphones across the room in an attempt to remove them from her head. "Deputy… can I help you?" Sarah asked in her usual flirtatious tone. "Did any calls come in from Glasford in the last hour or so?" Alan asked. "No you did not receive any calls deputy…" Sarah said innocently. "I am not talking about me; did anyone through your exchange receive a call from Glasford?" Alan asked with a stern tone.

Sarah looked down at the connections log and scanned the lines with her finger. "No, nothing from Glasford this whole afternoon," Sarah said as she closed the logbook. Alan loosened his posture then sat on the console next to the logbook. "Sarah are you sure there were no calls?" Alan asked as he stroked some loose strands of hair on the side of her head. Sarah closed her eyes for a brief pause, "I have been told not to…" Alan pulled a chair close to Sarah then sat down looking into her eyes. "Tell me, what are you not to tell me?" Alan asked softly. Sarah looked away from Alan, "I've been told never to tell... anyone... who made or received calls. It's getting late so I would like to eat dinner before the evening calls start."

Alan stood up and put the chair back. "Who owns the phone company?" Alan asked without hesitation. Sarah placed the headphones back on her head, "Charles Kiel." Alan looked closely at the switchboard to see each jack named as to whose phone it was for. On the top row, fourth from the left was the jack labeled as Kiel that still held a circuit plug. Sarah watched as Alan traced the rubber covered cable back to the switchboard base and a small brass plate label simply "Glasford A."

Alan smiled to Sarah, "Good evening Sarah." Sarah looked only with a blank stare and did not acknowledge Alan as he went down the stairs to the street. When the closing of the door was heard, she removed the Glasford circuit plug from the Kiel jack and placed in another plug. She spun a handle on the face of the switchboard and paused waiting for an answer. "Mister Kiel, its Sarah. You asked to let you know if Deputy Johnson ever came looking for information... he just wanted to know if anyone received a call from Glasford... No I did not tell him. Yes sir... good bye..." Sarah removed the plug from the jack and let the cable retract back into the base. "Thank you for help!" Alan said standing back in the doorway, "Next time make sure I actually went through the door before you call Charles." Sarah did not say a word. She just sat looking at the switchboard.

Alan's automobile was taking the ruts in the dry road with ease as he burned through the countryside on his way to Charles' farm. The farm was quiet as most of the day's work was completed and the men were at home with their families or sitting in a tavern. The car continued to roll a few feet after Alan jumped out, ran up the porch steps and opened the screen door without knocking. "Where are you Kiel?" Alan shouted.

The house was quiet, filled only with the sounds of crickets coming from outside. "Out here!" Came a voice from the rear of the house. Alan walked through the house to the kitchen and then finally to another screen door leading to a rear porch. Sitting on a white rocking chair was Charles with a pipe in his hand with a faint blue haze swirling around his head.

"Before you even say a word I will take care of my family myself," Charles said then took another puff on the pipe. "Take care of your family? The hell with you! I was actually feeling sorry for you, but you are nothing but a soulless man who only cares about himself." Alan said. "You need to understand boy, my farm is all I have. Yes, I have money, but this land is my legacy. I will not let someone pull it out from under me." Charles barked in his usual gruff tone.

Alan grabbed Charles by his collar, "Does protecting your legacy mean sending someone to threaten my girlfriend?" Charles tried his best to loosen Alan's grip, "I do not know what you are speaking of. I did not threaten anyone!" Alan only tightened his grip, "Then who sent that man to the restaurant this afternoon?" Charles face was deep red from anger and lack of oxygen. "I didn't…," managed to squeak out. Alan let go of Charles who was now coughing for breath. "Who sent him then? I know Lange called you…," Alan said.

Charles looked up to Alan, "Lange? The state's attorney? I didn't speak to him… What the hell are you talking about?" Alan looked down to the flustered old man, "If you did not speak to Lange who did? Someone at this house took the call!" Charles sneered back, "Well I did not speak to him. There was a call before but the ring was for Philip's house!" Alan eyes narrowed as what he just heard sunk in, "Philip?" Charles reached for a glass that was sitting next to his chair. He took a sip and started to cough again, "Yes! We are on a party line…"

Alan looked out to the pasture to see two horses running in the late afternoon sun. He could feel his heart beating in his ears and his head ached slightly. "I ran into Gordon Higgins at the general store this morning. He told me you were looking at the land deeds… He told me Philip is buying up all of the property surrounding mine," Charles said in a somber tone. "I think Philip killed Rebecca and Martha. For all I know he might have killed George also," Alan said, "but I think you already knew that."

Charles took a puff on his pipe so as to calm his nerves, "I didn't until today." Alan turned to Charles, "Does Philip have hired hands?" Charles shook his head in agreement, "Yes. He has about three or four men this time of year. He will hire six fold at harvest." Alan leaned against the railing, "You know I am going to take your son down. I have no way of proving he committed the murders, but if he sent that man to hurt Amie, I do not care…" Charles took another puff only to find the bowl empty, "You can take care of that man… I'll take care of Philip."

Chapter 14

Philip Kiel had a farm to rival his fathers in ways more than just acreage. He raised cattle, sheep and hogs. The farmhouse was new and built to a grand scale far beyond the dreams of a common farmer. Like most farmhouses in the area, it was built on a slight hill so as to overlook its fields. The barn that was slightly downhill from the house was large enough for all his animals and all the farm equipment the modern farmer required. However like his father, it was hired hands who did all of the work.

Alan stopped his automobile just south of the farmhouse at the side of a field of corn. The last thing he wanted was to be seen by either Philip or his men. With a pair of binoculars in hand, he made his way through the towering corn to a position where he hoped he could spy on the men working, however the placement of the barnyard made this impossible. He snuck quickly to the rear of the barn and made his way around the three concrete silos. As he rounded the last silo he saw a group of three men hoisting hay bales off of a wagon and into the barn under the hot morning sun. None of the men looked familiar to Alan and they did not match the description Amie gave.

Alan looked toward the house to see a woman and young girl sitting on the porch peeling potatoes. No one else was in sight and Alan decided to make his way back to the car before being spotted. If sneaking around would not give him the information he needed, he would drive up to the house and make his visit official. As Alan turned to sneak back he was confronted by the sight of a tall, thin man standing behind him. In the man's hand was a small revolver pointed right at Alan's face.

"Pull your gun out of your holster and throw it next to the barn," the man said in a very cold tone. Alan reached down slowly with his right hand, unbuttoned the leather strap and slid his gun out of its holster. Alan did not want to let go of the gun but knew he was dead for sure if he held on. He did as he was told and threw the gun onto the sun baked ground.

"You are taking quite a risk pulling a gun on a deputy sheriff," Alan said with an uneasy tone, "who are you?" The man just grinned with few discolored teeth then made a snorting noise and spit a wad of chewing tobacco at Alan's feet. "Come on… we'll go back the way you came in, nice and quiet like," the man said as he gestured with the gun. Alan walked slowly looking for anything he could disarm the man with. "I was hoping you would do something dumb like this… that little filly of yours, she's real pretty. It's sad you will not see her again," the man said as they started to enter the cornfield.

Alan forgot his circumstance and turned back to the man, "I figured you were the one. Philip Kiel send you?" The man placed the muzzle of the gun against Alan's forehead and said, "Turn around and walk back to the road or you will die right here…" Alan could feel his head start to hurt and the sound of his heart beating was becoming louder in his ears. His body wanted to turn as instructed but his mind was made to take down the man who threated Amie. "You city boys ain't too smart. You would think a gun to your head would make you listen better…" the man said as he pressed the muzzle into Alan's temple harder, "get moving!"

Alan was deciding if he was ready to die or fight hard for his life. He slowly stepped back and turned toward the road. The stalks of corn were taller than both men and obscured the view of the surrounding area. As Alan walked the man stayed closely behind with the gun pointing at Alan's head. Just as Alan emerged from the field into the clearing the road created, Alan heard a sharp thud that caused him to spin around. Alan looked to see the man on the ground and Kenneth Lynch standing with a large stone in his right hand.

"You okay deputy?" Ken asked. Alan looked at the man on the ground to see him holding his head with one hand and feeling the stalks with the other trying to find the dropped revolver. Just as his fingers started to feel the grip of the gun, Ken kicked the gun away then stepped on the man's hand.

"I saw your carriage sitting at the side of the road… I had called on Charles this morning. He told me about your visit last night," Ken said, "I figured you would get yourself into trouble…" Alan pulled a pair of handcuffs from his belt and placed them on the ailing man. "My gun is back at the barn. I better go get it," Alan said as he wiped sweat from his forehead with his arm, "can you keep an eye on him?" Ken placed his right foot on the man's stomach. "I'll keep an eye on him," Ken said with a broken smile.

Alan saw that his prisoner was in good, if not overly tense, hands and returned to the field. He quickly made it to the barn and as before peered around the silo to see where the workers were located. The woman was still on the porch peeling potatoes and the young girl's interest had turned to a tabby kitten. Alan went back around the silos to find his gun in the dirt. He bent over to pick it up just in time to hear a single shot ring across the fields.

Alan ran into the field toward where he left the men. He came through the stalks to see the man's gun in Ken's hand and the man's left shoulder bleeding. "What the hell happened?" Alan cried as he pulled the revolver from Ken's hand. "He kicked up at me and knocked me to the ground… luckily I got to the gun before he did. Then the little bastard tried to get it away from me… why did you cuff him with his hands in his front?!" Ken asked with his usual angered tone.

Alan ripped the man's shirt above the wound only to see the bullet barely nicked the skin.

"It's nothing, you're lucky Ken is a crack shot…," Alan said with a hint of humor. "My arms burning, I need doctoring!" the man said. "You don't need a doctor; I have a pint of alcohol at the house. That will make sure you don't get any infection." Ken said, "and the burn may make you think about what you did."

"Taking him by your house isn't a bad idea. He pretty much admitted he was the one who threatened Amie, but I want her to identify him," Alan said. "I threated no one… you all trying to pin something on me I didn't do!" the man said spitting like a snake. "And after she confirms he is the man, what will we do with him?" Ken asked. "We'll do nothing; I'll take him where no one will find him. I have a feeling our friend here knows much more than we think," Alan said as he pulled the man to his feet using his shirt collar.

Ken mounted his horse, "when you get to the house, park on the Vogal's property. I'll bring Amie over." Alan nodded his head in agreement and placed the man in his vehicle. "You have no idea the hornets you just poked at Deputy…," Alan heard from the back seat as he shifted the car into gear. "You have no idea friend…" Alan said dryly.

The car rumbled down the road as the man sat in the back seat yelling at Alan about anything he could. "Would you just shut up?!" Alan yelled as he slammed on the brakes causing the man to hit his head on the back of Alan's seat. "I think you knocked a tooth loose! You did that on purpose!" the man said. "I couldn't help it; there was a large rock in the road…" Alan said while trying not to laugh. "You think your funny friend. I only got five teeth left… You won't be laughing much longer. They'll come get me, you'll see!" the man shouted even louder as Alan parked the car. Alan got out, opened the rear door and grabbed the man by his collar, "Now, stand here and keep your mouth shut!"

Ken escorted Amie down the driveway toward the men. "I don't need to go any further… that's him… he's the one." Amie said trying not to cry. "You go back and help your mother. I'll let the deputy know." Ken stated while trying not to show his boiling anger. Ken's pace grew faster with every step he made toward the men. "It's him!" Ken said as he charged the man. He pulled the man away from Alan, threw him to the ground and started to kick him as he balled up on the grass. "Damnit stop!" Alan yelled as he tried his best to pull the angry father off of the handcuffed man.

"You better keep these chains on me… I kill both of you! I'll torch your houses! They'll burn just like this one did…" The man yelled as he laid on his right side still curled up in a ball. "What do you know about this house burning?" Alan asked as he kept Ken at bay. "Ain't know nothing… just saw the burned-out house… that's all." The man said carefully with a calmed voice, "what you going to do with me? You can't hold me forever!"

Alan pulled the man back up to his feet and leaned him against the car body, "You have nothing to worry about. I'll take good care of you as long as you tell me everything you know… you understand?" The man looked at Ken and then to Alan, "I know nothin' lawman… I do know you got yourself a pretty woman. She also has a very pretty sister… I like to look at them… I tugged my weed last night thinking about having both of them at the same time…" Alan once again had to hold Ken back as the man started to laugh with a fully belly.

"Give him to me deputy, I'll make sure he never hurts no one again," Ken said with a growl. "You can't hurt me old man! None of you will hurt me… but I'll hurt you… so help me I'll hurt you but your women… they will give me pleasure while I hurt them!" the man said with a hysterical laugh. Alan pushed Ken away and turned rapidly only to punch the man in the stomach as hard as he could. With a sharp groan the man bent over in pain and started to dry heave.

The man was did his best to regain his breath. "If you two are finished take me to jail already. Sooner I get there the sooner they come and get me," the man said as he tried to get back to his feet himself. "First of all, we are the only one who know where you are and you are not going to jail," Alan said with a smooth tone. "Yep, let's kill him…" Ken said eagerly. Alan looked at Ken then shook his head in disagreement. "No… You are not officially under arrest, but you are not free either. I will keep you out in the country where no one will find you. Then you will tell me all about Philip Kiel and the jobs you have performed for him…" Alan said, "Ken I do not want to move him until its dark. Can I keep him in your barn?" Ken looked at the man with extreme disgust, "You can keep him with the hogs. They smell better than he does…"

"You all can't keep me! There are laws… you should know that lawman," the man said while trying to shake Alan's grip. "Deputy, remember we need to tend to that wound…" Ken said with a sadistic tone, "I might even have some wood alcohol…" The man's eyes grew wide, "No! That's poison! Don't leave me with that man… he's crazier than me!" Alan tugged at the man's arm to get him moving toward Kenneth's farm, "Don't worry, he won't use wood alcohol on you."

The men walked into the barn. Even with the doors wide open the heat was oppressive and the smell was strong enough to taste. Kenneth took the lead and walked into a small room off to one side. "Take him in here… You can handcuff him to that pipe over there," Ken said. Alan uncuffed the man's right hand, ran the handcuff around the iron pipe and retightened the cuffs on the man's hand.

"Now, you won't be going anywhere," Alan said, "So what is your name?" The man looked at Ken who was leaning in the doorway wearing the face of an executioner and then to Alan. "Give me some water… I'm thirsty," he said with an angered tone. "Can you fetch him some water?" Alan asked at Ken who nodded in agreement.

"Now I asked you a simple question. What is your name?" Alan asked again. Ken returned with a steel ladle filled with water and held it to the man's lips. The man took a sip then spit it on the wood floor, "Where the hell you get that water?" Ken laughed, "The horse trough. If it's good enough for them it has to be good enough for a jackass." The man charged toward Ken but the steel pipe kept him firmly, "Call me a jackass will you? I'll gut you old man. I show you what your insides look like just before the devil takes your soul!" Ken looked at Alan who was looking back in amazement, "This boy is crazier than a shithouse rat!"

The man started to laugh hysterically again, "Maybe that's my name... Shithouse rat! Shithouse rat! Better than the name my mama gave me... Rene." Ken started to laugh, "Why... that a ladies name! No wonder you are crazy!" Rene tried to break free of the pipe again but to no avail. "I bet you were made fun of as a boy," Alan said with a chuckle. "That's right and I will remember you two making fun of me. You won't be laughing when they come free me... I'll be coming for both of you and your women," Rene said with venom.

"I need to get my chores done before lunch. You can stay here with girly Rene if you want," Ken said and started to laugh hardily at the crazed man. Alan shook his head in disbelief as Ken walked away.

181

"Okay Rene, what is your last name?" Alan asked calmly. "Ain't got no last name lawman… Been on my own since I was a boy. I watched my momma be passed around by men for money so I left. Must have been six, seven," Rene said with a somber tone.

"What city did you live in? Where have you lived?" Alan asked then sat down on a three legged milking stool. "Don't remember. It was in the south. I mostly traveled on the railroad. Hop on top of a boxcar and where it stopped I would stay for a bit. I take good care of myself," Rene said. "That how you got here? On the railroad?" Alan asked. "I was somewhere not far from here couple weeks back and the brakeman caught me taking some apples from a box car. He beat me upside the head and when I woke I was laying on the side of the tracks. I walked into town and some man asked me if I wanted some work…," Rene said while trying to rub his wrists where the cuffs were chafing.

"Who was the man?" Alan asked. "Don't matter and you ain't going to get me to say anything else. You gonna take me to jail or not?" Rene asked as his anger started to replenish. "No… you're not going to jail and you will tell me everything you know about Philip Kiel and his dealings," Alan said with a stern tone. "Don't know no Philip… Don't know nothing lawman. Well… maybe I do know something though…" Rene said as a large grin started to fill his dirty face. "What's that?" Alan asked.

Rene slumped down to the wood floor and started to giggle like a small child, "Yesterday… your filly smelled so nice, like flowers on a spring morning." Alan could feel his heart starting to beat in his ears again. "I ran my hand up her body… I felt every inch of her and then I felt her tits. They felt nice and firm like a young woman should have…" Rene said with a giggly, excited tone as he ran his hands up the steel pipe, "I wanted to take her flower right there… You never mounted her yet, have you?"

Alan felt something snap in his head as he jumped to his feet, picked up the stool and bashed it into Rene's skull. Without thinking he hit the laughing man again and was about to take another swing when a firm hand gripped his wrist. Alan turned his head rapidly to see Kenneth stopped his pummeling of the shackled man.

"One of Philips Kiel's hired hands just came by. He saw your buggy and wanted to speak with you. He's waiting out near the tool shed…" Ken said as he took the stool away from Alan. "What does he want?" Alan asked as he looked at Rene slumped on the floor with a thick trickle of blood slowing flowing down his forehead. "Don't know… I will put a gag in him to keep him quiet while you go talk with the man," Ken said.

Alan tried to calm himself before he walked out of the barn. As he walked into the blazing sun he saw a blond haired man holding the reins of a white horse. "Kenneth said you need to speak with me," Alan said. "Yes sir. I work for Mister Kiel, Philip Kiel. My name is Henry. We had a drifter come work with us. He disappeared this morning, but stole a gun and some money. I was hoping you may have seen him," the hired hand said in broken English. "What does he look like Henry?" Alan asked as Ken walked up into the conversation. "He is tall, thin with black hair and a thin mustache," Henry said. Ken looked to Alan. "No… no I have not seen anyone like that… If I do I will arrest him for theft," Alan said with a guiltless tone, "whose gun and money was it?"

Henry looked to the ground as if looking for an answer, "The money was mine, about ten dollars. The gun… the gun was Mister Kiel's." Alan gave a queer look to the hired hand, "Why did Mister Kiel not report the theft?" Henry shrugged his shoulders but did not answer. "What is the man's name?" Alan asked. "Don't know sir. He never told us. He has not worked with us too long. We needed more men to help put up the hay. He showed up one day to help," Henry said through a German accent that was getting thicker with each answer.

"He just showed up one day?" Alan asked. "Well… Mister Kiel brought him and told me to show him what to do… I need to get back to the farm sir, I will let Mister Kiel know that you will look for the drifter," Henry said then mounted his horse. "Yes… I will keep an eye out for him

Henry… Please tell Mister Kiel I will come calling on him this afternoon," Alan said calmly. "I'll do that sir," Henry stated.

As the men watched the hired hand ride down the driveway, Ken turned to Alan, "You think Kiel really wanted a police report taken?" Alan shook his head in disagreement, "No. But he does want that man because he knows a lot more than he is telling me. Can I keep him here? I think this might be the safest spot." Ken gave a look of displeasure, "Yes, but not in the barn. There is an old root cellar beneath the creamery; I do not want the girl's knowing he is here. I'll sneak food to him… give a bucket to crap in and some corn cobs…"

Alan looked up toward the house to see Amie looking down at him from an upper window, "Ken I want you to know that if Kiel or anyone for that matter ever tries to hurt Amie, I will take care of them like a man, not a lawman." Ken placed his left hand on Alan's shoulder, "I never had any doubt deputy…"

Chapter 15

The afternoon heat was giving way to building thunderheads as Alan stepped onto the front porch of Philip Kiel's house. Before he could raise his hand to knock, the door opened to revel a large woman who wore a head scarf and an apron dusted with flour. "Excuse me, I would like to speak with Mister Kiel," Alan said as he removed his hat from his head. "He's in his office. Please come into the sitting room and have a seat. Would you like some water or ice tea?" the woman asked. "No, no thank you. Um, may I ask, are you the Kiel's' cook?" Alan asked with curiosity.

The woman gave a small chuckle, "Yes sir! Been with the family for over fifteen years. Seen their daughters grow up into fine women…" As the woman spoke Alan remembered seeing the woman and young girl. It never crossed his mind that Philip's wife had left him and his children were grown. "Sir… sir?" the woman asked. "Oh sorry, I guess I… um… the heats been getting to me, I'm sorry," Alan said. "I'll go fetch Mister Kiel for you, please have a seat…," the cook said in a suspicious tone.

Alan sat on a red velvet seat and held his hat in his hand waiting for Philip Kiel to arrive. The minutes flew by as Alan listened to the wall clock tick in an annoying fashion. In the distance small rolls of thunder could be heard and the sounds of the men outside hurrying to bring in the animals before the storm arrived. Alan was dozing off from the constant ticking when the sound of heavy boots brought him back to life. "You want to see me deputy?" Philip Kiel announced as he walked into the room.

Alan stood up from the seat and turned to see Philip wearing a black suit and a blank expression. "Yes, I had one of your hands come see me this morning about the theft," Alan said. "Theft? What theft?" Philip said with innocence. "Henry said you had a gun taken and he had ten dollars lifted by a drifter you hired," Alan said with his voice starting to stress. "Deputy, I have no hand named Henry and sure as hell never hired no drifter. Now unless you have something else to waste my time on, I have work to do!" Philip barked.

"Now look Mister Kiel. I had a man with a thick German accent come to me and tell me he was your hired hand. Tell me, do you or do you not have a hired hand named Henry?" Alan asked with anger.

Philip walked to a window that looked out toward the barn, "Come here deputy… do any of those men look like the one who came to see you?" Alan walked over to see two men corralling the cows into the barn. "No. You only have two hands?" Alan asked with skepticism. "This time of year, yes. At the harvest I hire migrants, but I never hire no drifters and never had a hand named Henry. Now that you have wasted my time deputy, I will ask that you leave!" Philip said with a firm tone, "You know where the door is, let yourself out."

Alan walked through the door and out onto the porch as the sound of the approaching storm was trumpeting its arrival. Alan stepped off of the porch not to go to his car but to go toward the barn to greet the hands who just shut the barn door. "Gentlemen, I am Deputy Johnson. I would like to speak to you about a co-worker," Alan said in an official tone. The men looked at one another with uneasiness. "Have either of you talked with Henry today?" Alan asked. "Henry? Sir, we never worked with no Henry…," one man said smoothly.

"A man with blond hair and a thick German accent? You never worked with him?" Alan asked as he noticed one of them looking past him toward the house. Alan turned to see Philip standing on the porch with his arms folded. "Sir we need to get back to work," the other hand said. "Yes, you better get back to work before the skies open…" Alan said feeling defected once again.

Alan made his way back to his car as large droplets of rain start to fall in random areas. "Deputy!" Philip yelled dryly from the porch, "Next time you see Sheriff Bonner… say hello for me, won't you?" Alan did not say a word but just tipped his head in acknowledgment. The beating of his heart was back in his ears and his muscles twitched from the burning anger inside of him.

Alan stayed just ahead of the storm as he drove as quickly as he could back to town. He walked into the restaurant to get a cup of coffee and hopefully see Amie. To his displeasure Amie was not behind the counter, but instead Robin was manning the restaurant. "Did Amie go over to the general store?" Alan asked calmly. "No, she asked that I take over for her for a few days... you should know why...," Robin said with an angered tongue. "Yeah, I did see her this morning at the farm, I guess I should have figured she would not be here...," Alan said softly.

"What are you and pa up to?" Robin asked bluntly. "Up to? What do you mean?" Alan asked innocently. "Amie said you and pa went to Glasford together and then you were with him at the farm this morning... Since when do you two get along so well?" Robin asked as she poured a cup of coffee. Alan picked up the bowl of sugar cubes in anticipation of the coffee only to see Robin take a sip. "Oh, did you want a cup?" Robin asked. "Ah yes, I would like a cup... Robin, your father and I have come to an understanding... Men can do that you know..." Alan stated as Robin placed a cup of coffee down on the counter. Alan threw a few cubes of sugar in and watched them slowly dissolve into the blackness.

Robin looked out to see sheets of rain pummeling the dirt streets into puddles of muddy water. Just down the street at Alan's office a car had stopped and man got out only to find the door locked. "Deputy… someone is at your door… looks like he just got back into the car," Robin stated in a curious tone. "I wonder who the hell that is," Alan said softly while sipping the hot coffee. "Don't know, but he just spotted your car and looks like he is getting out here," Robin said while grabbing a clean coffee cup in anticipation.

The door swung open assisted by the wind driven rain. Two men walked in and did their best to shake the rain off before walking further into the restaurant. Alan did not turn but stayed looking at Robin until a familiar voice came from one of the men that made Alan close his eyes in disbelief, "Deputy Johnson?" Alan turned on the stool, his cup of coffee firmly in his hand, "Yes Sheriff…"

Sheriff Bonner removed his coat and hat then placed them on one of the wooden tables. "May we speak with Deputy Johnson alone?" the sheriff asked in Robin's direction. "Yes… I will be in the kitchen… just holler if you need anything," Robin said in a cautious tone. "Deputy Johnson this is Deputy Arlo Dunay… he will taking your post for the next two weeks starting now," the sheriff said as he sat next to Alan. Deputy Dunay eagerly extended his right hand to Alan only to have it left hanging in air.

"What is this about?" Alan asked trying not to show his displeasure. "Alan you have never taken a vacation, never took time off of work even when you had influenza last winter… you need a rest. This job grinds you down quickly and it makes your mind cloudy. That will affect your judgment…," the sheriff said with a tone of fatherly advice.

Alan took another sip of coffee then placed the cup on the counter, "So who feels I need a time out?" Sheriff Bonner raised his eyebrow and half rolled his eyes, "I do. I think you need to rest your body and take your mind off of this job. Go fishing, sleep in… hell go back to Chicago and visit your kin…." Before Alan could reply Robin chimed in through the kitchen door, "Marry your girlfriend…" Alan looked at the door then back to the sheriff and shook his head, "So no one came to you and asked that I be removed me from my post?"

Bonner looked to deputy Dunay, "It looks like the rain has stopped, why don't you take a walk around the stores. Meet some of the residents." The new deputy acknowledged with a nod of the head and went to the door but turned quickly, "Sir… what should I say if they ask where Deputy Johnson is?" The sheriff rubbed his goatee and made a sight growl, "Have you not been standing there for the last five minutes? Tell them he is on vacation for two weeks! Now go!" The timid deputy felt for the knob of the door but kept missing it. "If you turned toward the door, the knob would be easier to find…," Alan said with a dry humor. Turning to find the knob, Dunay made his way out into the steamy air.

"Well at least you are replacing me with someone who will show just how good I am," Alan said bluntly. "Lange complained quite vividly, said you and some dirt farmer came to see him with a bullshit story demanding that you needed to interview Philip Kiel," the sheriff said with a raised tone. "Oh he did… did he also tell you how he then called Philip Kiel who sent a drifter to threaten my girlfriend and her family. Did he also say how the drifter is now missing and for all I know is part of the murders and burning of the Vogal farmhouse?" Alan yelled.

"I am sure you have proof of all of this?" Bonner asked, his face turning red. "Concrete… no. But the pieces are coming together," Alan said. "I told you to tread lightly but you step like a pack mule and are just as stubborn. Listen to me… you are taking two weeks off and I do not want you anywhere near the Kiel's," the sheriff said with a stiff tone.

Alan pulled his revolver and placed it on the counter. Next he removed his badge and placed it with the gun. "You do not need to do that deputy, this is just a vacation. However your replacement will need to use the REO," the sheriff said. Alan grabbed the badge and gun then stood up, "I can live without the car, but here are the keys to the office and gun cabinet. He'll need them…," Alan said. Sheriff Bonner took the keys and stood up from the stool, "I'll give these to Dunay… I think he will know how to use them…," the sheriff said with a hint of humor, "enjoy your time off!"

Alan leaned against the counter as the sheriff left the restaurant. As the door to the restaurant closed, the door to the kitchen opened. "Deputy… I'm sorry… well at least you can spend your time with Amie…," Robin said trying to cheer up the simmering deputy. "I don't know how I will get to your farm to see Amie," Alan said with a disgusted tone. "I am sure pa will loan you one of our horses," Robin said trying not to laugh. Before Alan could respond the telephone rang. Robin picked up the receiver and as she starting to answer a voice came screaming through loud enough for Alan to hear across the room.

"Hold on he's right here… Hey whose phone are you using? Okay, okay… Alan, its pa!" Robin said flustered. Alan took the receiver from Robin who made sure to stay within ear shot. "Hello Ken…," Alan said before being cut off quickly by Kenneth. "I need you out at the farm… I had a problem with the creamery and only you can fix it," Ken said. "The what? Why would you need…? Um, I will be there as soon as I can," Alan said while trying to think of how he will get to the Lynch farm. "Hey whose phone are you using??" Alan asked puzzled. "What does it matter get over here now!" Ken yelled just before the line clicked off.

"So your father needs my help. I wonder if I can borrow a horse from the blacksmith," Alan said thinking out loud. "No, no need to do that. My horse is tied up under the lean-to out back. This place is dead anyways, let's head home," Robin said as she locked the cash register. Alan was looking nervous as Robin ran around closing the restaurant for the night. "Well come on already!" Robin said. They walked out behind the restaurant to find the horse finishing the last of his hay and swatting flies with his tail.

"Um, I've never been on a horse before," Alan said in a whisper to Robin. "Well you're in luck; I have the saddle on him. Usually I just ride bareback. I'll let you mount him first. Just put your left foot in the stirrup and use the horn to pull yourself up," Robin said as she was untying the reins from a wooden post with an iron loop. Alan did as was told but started to feel very uneasy as the horse started to walk backwards, "Hey… what the hell!"

Robin started to laugh, "You sure are a city boy… Now move onto his back. I need to sit on the saddle." Alan did as he was told trying to show bravery. As soon as Robin mounted the horse it started to move and was ready for the ride home. "Um, I am sliding off… I think I am going to fall off!" Alan yelled like a scared child. "Well grab on to me and hold tight!" Robin yelled back. Alan wrapped his arms around Robin's waist loosely. "If you want to stay on the horse, you better hold me a little tighter. Just imagine I am Amie," Robin said with humor. Alan did as he was told and tightened his grip. He did not realize that one sister would feel so much like another. "Um, not so tight there deputy," Robin said with a giggle.

They rode to the house at a pace far slower than Robin would usually take. Sitting on the porch of the house was a very nervous Kenneth and his latest whittling project. "Where the hell is your car? Why are you riding on the horse with Robin and get your arms away from her waist!" Kenneth yelled like a mad man, "Robin, put your horse up then wash for dinner." Alan tried his best to get off the horse without help and fell right into Grace's lilac bush. Alan stood to his feet and knocked the dirt off of his pants. Robin walked the horse to the barn trying not laugh out loud at the deputy's antics.

"What happened?" Alan whispered to Ken. "Come with me to the creamery," Ken said with urgency. The men walked into the wooden shed where the trapdoor to the storm cellar was wide open. "Where is Rene?" Alan asked. "I came out with some scraps for the hogs and saw the door open. I came down to find... find that...," Ken said pointing down to the dirt floor. Alan walked down the wooden steps to the corner of the stone foundation that held an eyelet and Alan's handcuffs.

"How did he get loose? Did you not tighten them tightly?" Alan yelled up to Kenneth. "Look at the floor below the cuffs," Ken said. The light in the storm shelter was dim but Alan could see something that looked like ground meat. "Oh my God, is that what I think it is?" Alan asked then made a gagging

195

noise. "I think he chewed enough of his hand off to get it loose of the cuffs." Ken said as his stomach was quickly souring. "Well he still had enough of his teeth," Alan said under his breath.

"Kenneth, dinner!" Grace yelled from the rear porch. "Come on… have dinner with us. Amie would love to see you I'm sure," Kenneth said as Alan walked up the steps, his coloring off. "Ken before we go in, something happened this afternoon. I have been placed on leave for two weeks," Alan said. "Why?" Ken asked, "I mean… what the hell are we going to do? That maniac is loose and he said he would come for my girls!"

Alan took a deep breath of the humid air to calm his rolling stomach then said quietly, "Lange complained to the sheriff. So I was told to take vacation for two weeks. He even brought some greenhorn in to take my place. I have much more to tell you, but let's go have dinner and act like nothing is wrong…" Ken shut the door to the creamery, "You will be cleaning that up after dinner I hope you know." Alan did not say a word but the growl from his stomach spoke volumes.

Grace was not expecting company so the dinner was not very formal and served on the small table in the kitchen. Alan sat next to Amie who was rather quiet for most of the dinner as was Alan and Kenneth. "Alan how was your day? Catch any desperate criminals?" Grace asked trying to start a conversation. Robin looked to Alan who looked to

Amie with his head held a little low. "Ah no, actually I am on vacation for the next two weeks," Alan said with a somber tone. "Really a whole two weeks off to do as you wish? That sounds so nice... what will you do?" Grace asked with excitement. Before Alan could reply Kenneth piped up, "He will be staying with us."

Alan looked to Kenneth who looked back with a slight scowl. "Really?" Amie asked. "Um... yes... your father asked if I would help out on the farm and well... I could never say no. Besides it may give Amie and me some time together...," Alan said with a wink to Amie. Ken bit his lip hard enough to draw blood.

"We will hitch up the wagon after dinner so we can go pick up some items from his house," Ken said with a fake smile, "we can put him up in the attic. Our old bed is still up there." Grace gave a queer look, "Ken, its hot up there... he will swelter in this heat!" Ken shrugged his shoulders, "Well there are only three bedrooms and he isn't sleeping with any of us!" Amie blushed with what her father said and Alan looked off into space causing Robin to giggle.

"Amie will sleep with Robin and Alan can sleep in Amie's room," Grace said with authority, "Now that is settled... how about some huckleberry pie for dessert?" Ken wiped his mouth with a cloth napkin, "Save some for us. I want to go pick up his clothes before it gets any later." Alan looked disappointed to have to wait for pie. "We'll try to save some," Grace said with a smile. Ken grabbed Alan by his right shoulder, "Come on, let's go hitch up the wagon." Alan wiped his mouth, "This should be interesting… learning to ride a horse and hitch up a wagon all in one afternoon."

The men walked out onto the porch into the cooling evening air. Ken pulled a cigarette from his shirt pocket and struck a match on the one of the white porch posts. He slowly took a drag on the cigarette while Alan waited for his lesson in wagon hitching. "Well… what are we waiting for?" Alan asked in impatience. "I always have a cigarette after dinner… hold your horses," Ken barked. "Um, not that I am complaining, but why did you tell your family I will be staying here for my vacation?" Alan asked.

"There is a maniac loose and we are the only ones who know about it. He said he would hurt my family… I need you here to help protect them…," Ken said with clenched teeth, "one only wonders how the hell you because a deputy..." Alan just rolled his eyes at yet another put down. Ken started to walk down the stairs but stopped and turned back to Alan, "Oh, if I catch you and my daughter in her room at the same time, I will tie you to the windmill… the blades not the tower."

Chapter 16

The sound of crickets in the night air was almost deafening as Alan and Amie enjoyed the cool evening. They sat closely on the green porch boards looking up into the stars just visible through the haze. "Amie, this vacation was not really planned but I am glad I will be able to see you more," Alan said softly. Amie moved closer and leaned back against his body. "Robin told me about the sheriff visiting. Alan, you do need a break. I mean, I want you to enjoy life. I have seen this case or whatever you call it taking a toll on you," Amie said while staring out to the crescent moon just rising about the cornfield.

Alan placed his arm around Amie's stomach and pulled her even closer still. "I always wanted to be a police officer. My father was an officer and so were all of my uncles. There was no doubt to what I would do with my life. However lately I wonder if this is who I want to be," Alan said in a somber tone, "Maybe I need a change and while I was so angry with Sheriff Bonner this afternoon, now I almost feel relieved." Alan realized Amie was starting to doze off. He kissed her on the top of her head then whispered, "Amie I love you so very much…"

Alan was interrupted by the screeching of the screen door. "Hey city boy, we get up early on the farm. You better hit the sheets or you will be of no use to me tomorrow," Ken said sternly. "Pa?" Amie said, "Go to bed yourself. Mom is waiting for you."

Ken grunted as he let the screen door slam shut and went up to bed. "I can't believe he lets you talk to him like that," Alan said with a chuckle. Amie shook her head and started to laugh, "Talk about disbelief, you two are acting like long lost friends!" Alan felt a little uneasy at her comment, "You're the one who wanted me to talk to him more…" Amie looked up at Alan, "Yes I did. Now I guess we both better get to bed. I put water in the wash basin and there is a towel on the hook next to it for you."

Alan helped Amie to her feet, "I will be up in a minute. I need to go to the, um, well the…" Amie giggled, "It's called the privy. It's okay to say privy in mixed company, honey. Just make sure to use the right side, pa said we have been favoring the left side too much…"

Alan gave her a look like she was an alien from space, "Um, yes… I will do that." Amie started to laugh, "My father is right, you are a city boy. I hope one day we will have a farm of our own but I guess it will need indoor plumbing!" Alan blushed a bit from Amie's ribbing, "If it doesn't, I will survive." Amie reach forward and kissed him on the lips then said, "Just remember that when winter comes. Good night Alan."

Alan leaned against a porch post and watched Amie walk into the house. He stepped down to the stone walkway and made his way to the privy. With every step he felt as if someone was walking with him. The privy was a small wooden building on a downslope from the house and near the shelterbelt. Alan could feel his senses were starting to overreact to every sound he heard, every shadow he saw in the darkness.

Just as he started to pull the door open, a voice came from behind, "Do you want the first watch or the second?" Alan spun around to see Ken holding a shotgun across his chest. "You just scared the shit out of me!" Alan said with excitement. "Well you are at the right place… I'll let you have the first watch. It will be easier for us to do this without Grace finding out. I'll be down about two," Ken said in a soft whisper. Alan shook his head in disbelief, "You make it sound like we are in the middle of a Zane Grey novel. That drifter is miles from here by now. I'll stay up a bit and read, but I am not worried so neither should you…"

Ken ground his teeth so as to not explode at his house guest, "Just keep one of the rifles with you and if you hear anything, make sure you know what you are shooting at. I don't want any of my cows turned to ground beef." Alan swiftly grabbed the rifle from Ken, "Don't worry and don't sneak up on me ever again!" The sound of a screech owl caused Ken to jump a bit. "You are wound too tight. You need a snort to calm down…," Alan said with a hint of humor. Ken stood still with an expressionless face. "Good night… pa," Alan said with snicker. Alan walked into the privy and as the door closed he heard Ken state, "Use one of the cobs, the Sears catalog is mine!"

Ken walked into the house to find his eldest daughter waiting for him. "It's nice that you asked Alan to stay, but can you please be a little more relaxed around him? Did you really need to follow him to the outhouse?" Amie asked with a stern tone. "I just wanted to make sure he didn't fall in… Listen, I like him and I want to get to know him better. Let me just do it in my own way," Ken said. "Okay, but just relax a bit," Amie said, "Good night pa, see you in the morning." Ken hugged his daughter then followed her up the wooden stairs. Just as they topped the landing, the sound of the slamming screen door made Ken jump. Amie looked at Ken like he was on fire, "It's just Alan coming back in, calm down!"

Alan laid on Amie's bed succeeding at not falling asleep. He was tired, but the day's events were replaying time and time again in his mind. The windows were wide open allowing a cool, but damp breeze to flow in as well as the sounds of insects singing. Alan rolled onto his left side and looked out one of the windows into the late summer darkness. The bed smelled of Amie and it was adding to the emotions swirling around his head.

Alan's eyes were growing heavier and slowly he started to nod off when a sound caused his eyes to pop back open. He listened carefully and through the sounds of the crickets was a whistle, not the whistle of the breeze blowing through the windows nor the whistle of a distant train. It was the musical whistle of man. Alan hopped out of the bed and looked out into the darkness. Along with the whistle was now the sound of boots walking down the road. Alan grabbed the shotgun and as quietly as he could he sneaked down the steps. He went out onto the rear kitchen porch then proceeded around the side of the house.

Alan's eyes had adjusted to the darkness and the figure of a tall, thin man on the road became quite evident. The whistling had stopped as did the steps. Alan could not make it any further toward the road without being seen by the man. The man stood in the middle of the road looking not at the Lynch farm but toward the Vogal farm. Alan watched as the man walked toward the burned out foundation that was now surrounded by knee high grass and weeds.

Alan sneaked down the hill to the road, crossed over and hid behind one of the trees in the yard. The first sound of the man's voice told Alan who it was. "He told me you'd try to get me!" Rene yelled to the black hole in the ground. Alan did not know if Rene knew he was behind him so he did not make a sound. "I got you... you didn't think I would do it either did you?" Rene said this time with more anger in his voice, "You burned... I burned you and you still talk to me! You all still talk to me… stop! I did what he told me… you still scream in my sleep!" Alan watched the mentally defective man collapse down to his knees while grabbing his ears as if in great agony.

Alan felt something moving next to his bare foot. He looked down to see it was a garden snake taking a liking to his toes. The city boy was about to come out in him and he was doing his best not to make a sound as the snake inspected his feet. Rene stood back up and raised his right hand to revel a dirty white bandage, "Look what I had to do. The lawman tried to stop me, but he didn't. I'm gonna get him also… get his woman. I'm gonna make her love me like she loves him. The lawman tried to get you, he couldn't… but I could! You killed her and I loved her… but I burned you, didn't I? I heard your soul scream, I still hear it! Your soul walks around this house screaming of the pain you caused…"

Alan was trying to control his breathing, tried to stay completely still. Rene walked to the windmill and dunked his head in the trough. He then dunked his bandaged hand into the water and howled like an injured animal. It was so loud Alan knew for sure Kenneth and the women had to of heard it. Alan watched the madman as he sat on the edge of the trough holding his mangled hand and was crying into the night. Alan was readying himself to capture Rene when a hand came from behind, grabbed Alan's mouth and held tight. "It's me, stay quiet," Ken whispered. He let go and Alan quietly turned to see not just Kenneth but also Charles Kiel.

"How much did you hear?" Alan whispered. "We heard it all. Charles has been following him since he went past his place," Ken said. Charles stared at the madman who was now falling asleep at one foot of the steel tower holding the windmill. "So what should we do?" Ken asked of the two men. Charles pulled a chrome Colt pistol from his pants pocket, "He just confessed to killing my boy. He needs to pay for what he did." Alan reached forward and grabbed Charles' hand. "No, he said he loved her and he killed her. I think he means he loved Rebecca and George killed her, but that can't be." Ken gestured to Alan to lower his voice, "Why can't that be?"

"He told me he came here only a few weeks back. He could have not seen her let alone fall in love with her," Alan said softly. "The man is nuts, who is to say when he truly came here. Hell, he may have been here for years!" Charles said excited, "No jury in the world would convict me... just walk away, both of you. This is my war not yours." Alan quickly pulled the gun from the elderly man's hand. "God damn it, give me the gun back!" Charles shouted. Rene grunted at the noise but went right back to sleep. "Ken, go get some rope. We will tie him up," Alan said with authority.

Ken ran across the road and up his driveway. "What will you do with that idiot?" Charles asked, his voice stressing. "I think he did kill George. I know for a fact he threatened Amie and I am also sure he wants to kill Ken and me. However, this is not of his own doing. I think someone is using his warped mine to control him. Make him think we are out to hurt him," Alan said.

Charles ran his right hand through his sweaty white hair, "Who do you think that person is?" Ken returned with the rope and handed it Alan. "The same person who I really think killed the women, your son Philip," Alan said. Charles leaned back against the tree, closed his eyes and sighed.

Alan took the rope and slowly snuck through the tall weeds toward the madman under the windmill. Like a cowboy rustling a calf, Alan hog tied Rene in one swift move. "He didn't even wake up!" Ken said with astonishment. "He's burning up. That hand is bleeding right through the bandages, he might be going septic," Alan said. Rene moaned then opened his eyes to see the three men looking down at him. "It's you!" Rene exclaimed as he struggled to get free, "I was coming to get you and you too old man… and you too!" Alan looked to Charles whose eyes were bulged out with surprise.

"You know Charles?" Alan asked of Rene who was trying his best to rip the ropes apart. "I know him… oh I know him. I was going to pay him a visit after I ripped you two apart and loved your women until they could not love no more…" Ken clenched his teeth and in one swift move kicked Rene in his wounded hand causing the mental defect to scream in pain again. Alan grabbed Ken by his shoulder and pulled him away from the wounded man.

"How do you know him?" Alan asked as he pointed to Charles. "I saw his picture; he told me he would hurt me so I should hurt him first… I was coming to hurt him. I was going to pull his tongue out and wrap it around his neck! Untie me lawman and I will show you what I want to do to all of you!" Rene exclaimed.

"Where did you see a picture of me?" Charles asked flustered. Rene stayed quiet except for a low, painful moan. "I need doctoring, but he would not help me… I asked him, but he said I had more work to do before I could be doctored," Rene said as he started to cry. "There are no photographs of me… except…," Charles started to state, then turned quiet. Ken looked over to Charles, "except what?" Charles looked down to Rene, "Who else was in the photograph, boy?" Rene rolled in the grass trying again to untie the ropes. "God damn it look at me! Who else was in the photograph?" Charles asked with renewed anger.

Rene sat up and as he looked to the ground, rubbed the rope against the angle iron leg of the windmill. Charles bent over the struggling lunatic, "Look at me boy! Tell me who was in that photograph." Rene looked up; his eyes dark like the night sky, "Bunch of people. Men and their… their women… some children… I like little children… they don't hurt you like grown-ups!" Alan shook his head in disbelief. "He was in the picture, his woman was with him. I loved her as soon as I saw her and he… he killed her!" Rene exclaimed with venom. Charles had a look of astonishment on his face. "You know that photograph?" Alan asked. Charles shook his head in agreement, "Yes. I am only in one photograph. About three years ago we had a family photograph taken on the lawn at my house. Each of us has a copy…"

"Where did you see this photograph?" Alan asked Rene. "It was on the mantle," Rene said innocently, "please… please take me to the doctor. I feel like the devil is in my blood." Alan knelt down and looked Rene in the eyes, "We'll get you to the doctor, but you need to tell me whose mantle that photograph is on." Rene started to cry, "Please take me for doctoring… please!" Charles' anger was being visible enough to make Kenneth nervous.

"Rene, tell me whose mantle has that photograph," Alan said. "His mantle… he told me who to take care of. Who wanted to hurt me… He told me if I hurt them, they could not hurt me! He told me! He promised! My hand… I can't feel it no more. You made me do this to my hand! You and that old man… I'm gonna take it out on your women. They gonna love me and I'll make you watch!"

"I can't take any more of this! We all know whose mantle that photograph is on, it's Philips," Charles said with great anger, "the mantle, it is oak with carved flowers?" Rene looked up, "Yes... pretty flowers. They looked like the flowers that used to be in my mama's hair... she would wear flowers in her hair when the men would take turns at her..." Ken shook his head in disbelief, "That's enough. I'll go hitch up the wagon and we can get him to Doc Wright." Charles walked off toward the stone foundation and broke down sobbing. "I'll be back with the wagon," Ken said to Alan, "see what you can do to calm Charles down." Alan walked off and placed his right hand on the old man's shoulder.

Ken walked up toward his house to see Grace standing on the porch waiting for him. "I knew you two were up to something," Grace said, "is it finally over? So much pain has infected this community because of that family." Ken shrugged his shoulders, "There is much you do not know but this is not the time to talk about it. Go back in the house and lock the doors. We need to take someone to the doctor, might not be back until daylight."

Grace stepped toward Ken and hugged his tightly, "You better be back you old S-O-B." Ken wrapped his arms around her and hugged her tight, "I'll be back honey." Grace walked into the house and closed the door behind her. Sitting on the stairs both girls were waiting with impatience. "You two go back to bed, whatever is going on, the men are taking care of it," Grace said.

Chapter 17

"What the hell happened to him?" Doctor Wright asked as the men carried Rene into the doctor's house. "He's a lunatic, bit most of his hand off," Ken said dryly. "Please help me doc… I have a job to do… There are people who want to hurt me… I gotta git them…," Rene said softly; his eyes barely open with sweat pouring down his face. The doctor loosened the bandage to see the mangled hand then looked up to Alan and shrugged his head toward the parlor. The men walked in to the room dimly lit by a single Edison bulb. "That man is very sick," the doctor said. "Hell I could have told you that…," Ken said in a cross tone.

"You do not understand, that hand is very infected. His only chance is to have it removed, but judging by his fever his blood is already poisoned. I cannot do the operation here, but I do not think he can make the trip to Glasford. I will give him an injection of morphine for the pain," the doctor said. "So he has no chances, does he?" Alan asked. "No… I'm afraid not, do you know if he has any local kin?" the doctor asked as he grabbed a pad of paper and pencil. "He's indigent and has no one that I know of," Alan said, "they have a potter's field in Glasford…" The doctor placed the items back on his desk, "So sad, he looked like a healthy young man otherwise." Ken smirked, "His body may have looked healthy, but his mind has been diseased for years."

"Doctor, you can remove the ropes, I do not think he is of much danger any longer," Alan said. "No, he will not be for sure once I give him the morphine," the doctor said bluntly, "why don't you two go. I will take care of the patient." Alan shook his head in agreement, "We need to get back anyway. Thank you for your help doctor. I'll check in later this afternoon." The doctor opened a glass fronted wooden cabinet to get the powerful pain medication, "He will be in the hands of Heath and Knilge by then…" The men did not acknowledge what the doctor just said and left him to his duty.

Kenneth and Alan walked down the steps of the doctor's house to see Charles sitting on the bench of the wagon staring into space. "So what do we do now?" Ken asked. Charles stayed quiet and motionless. "Why don't we take Charles back home," Alan said. "No… we are going to see Philip," Charles piped up. "You sure about that?" Ken asked cautiously. "He's my boy and I am responsible for how he turned out. Maybe if I held a firmer hand to him when he was younger, he would have not done what he has," Charles said in a slow, somber tone, "Maybe the women… and George would still be alive. I need to make sure he never does this again."

Alan shook his head in disagreement, "I'm a deputy, I'm not the judge and jury…" Ken stopped

Alan quickly, "Don't! Don't you dare give a lecture right now. What Philip did was bad enough then he decided to send a madman to come after my daughter. I thought you loved her… a real man would go after anyone who hurts the woman he loves!" Alan was torn between his duty as a deputy and his pride. "Fine, but I will be arresting him when we are done," Alan said sternly. "I hope you don't expect him to go willingly," Charles said, "his mother always said he had a thick skull… just like me. I am sure he will take all three of us on. I'm glad that Caroline did not live to see the shambles our boys have become. Michael seems to be the only straight one, but he no longer speaks with me." The men watched as Charles' held his head low again and wept.

The horizon was starting to glow a light yellow from the rising sun. The air was damp and the smell of earth was pungent as the men rode to Philip Kiel's farm. Kenneth stopped the wagon just down the road from their destination. "What are you stopping for?" Charles asked. "Alan hand me that small crate," Ken said pointing to an old wooden box at Alan's feet. Ken opened the box and pulled out a pair of pliers. "What are you up to?" Alan asked while Ken jumped off of the wagon and walked into the grass. "I want to make sure Charles' boy cannot call anyone for help." Ken walked up to a wooden telephone pole and climbed the steel rungs pounded into the sides of it. "There's

212

electricity up there, you sure you know what you're doing?" Charles asked. "Yea I think he knows what he is doing judging by this telephone he has with his tools…," Alan said with a hint of humor, "Now I know how you called me yesterday." Charles scowled, "Climbing poles to make free calls… I'll remember to send you a bill!"

Ken looked down at Charles and shook his head in disbelief. He reached over to one of two wires being supported by amber colored glass insulators and snipped it with the pliers. The wire snapped back toward the next pole like a spring then fell to the grass. "There, now your boy can't call any of his paid friends in Glasford," Ken said. Alan just looked at Ken in amazement as he climbed back down the pole. "I'll make sure to send you the bill for the repair also," Charles said. "Don't worry, I'll fix it for ya," Ken said with a thin smile.

The roosters were crowing as the sun started to top the fields of corn as they came to the farm. Except for the crowing rooster the farm looked deserted. "They should be milking the cows right now," Ken said quietly. "What would Philip be doing?" Alan asked Charles. "Doing? Sleeping. He never got up early for anything. That is what the hands are for," Charles snapped back. "Ken, stop the wagon out here, we will walk the rest of the way to the house," Alan said.

As they dismounted the wagon, the barn door swung open with a large squeak causing the

213

men to take notice. "Ken, look who just walked out of the barn… Henry." Alan said then gestured for the hired hand to come talk to him. Henry looked around then jogged over to the men. "Sir, you should not be here," Henry said. "Why did Philip tell me he never heard of you… you've been in a fight…" Alan said when he noticed the man's fair skin bruised. Henry looked nervously toward the farmhouse.

"What happened?" Alan asked. "Please, I do not want any trouble. I just need to work and take care of my family," Henry said. "You have a wife and I am guessing a little girl," Alan stated. "Yes… I need to get to work, good-bye," Henry said with haste as his thick accent took over. The hired hand ran back to the barn just as one of the other men came out looking for him.

"Well lets go wake your boy up and get this over with," Alan said as his anger was building. Charles walked up the steps and groaned as his knee cracked from arthritis. He reached forward, turned the brass door knob and slowly opened the stiff wooden door. The men walked in to find Philip waiting for them. He sat in the red velvet chair, a rifle across his lap and an empty bottle of whisky at his feet.

"I see you fools just walk right into a man's home without knocking," Philip said, his voice slightly slurred. Alan started to open his mouth to talk, but Kenneth stopped him. "This is Charles' fight, let him talk," Ken whispered. "You send that madman out to kill us?" Charles asked. "What madman?" Philip asked. "We're beyond games boy, you start telling the truth!" Charles barked.

Philip placed his hands on the rifle and started to laugh, "You think you know me, don't you? You don't know nothing old man!" Charles stood his ground in front of his eldest son, "I started you out, I started all my boys out in life. Look around, you've done good… What did I do to you to cause your anger?" Philip reached down for the bottle of whisky only to find it empty. "You're nothing but a rummy. Your daughters want nothing to do with you and your wife left you," Charles stated, "I have no idea why you turned to the bottle, but it seems to be your best friend. Your wife loved you and your daughters looked up to you like you were a god, but you threw them away for that God damn bottle!"

From a side door, Philip's cook came in looking to see what all the yelling was about, "Everything good?" Alan put his hand up telling the cook to stop where she was. "Does any of you gentlemen want some breakfast? I have biscuits baking, should be ready in ten minutes," Belle said hoping to defuse the situation. Ken raised his left hand, "I could go for a biscuit and some honey…" Alan looked at Ken with a face of displeasure. "Maybe I better not, thank you for the offer," Ken said with disappointment. "Belle get your black ass back in the kitchen and stay there!" Philip yelled.

215

"Um, yes, sir…" Belle said as she looked to the floor and swiftly left for the kitchen.

"All of you leave my house. I did what I had to do to be the best! To be the man my father kept telling me I wasn't… I now have the largest farm in Park County… larger than the former title owner, Charles Kiel," Philip said with pride, "I did it all by myself with no help from my old man." Charles' anger reached the boiling point, "You think being better than me is all life is about? You think having hundreds of acres makes you a better husband or father? That is what you should be concerned with! Where are your daughters? Where is your wife? They sure the hell aren't here!"

Philip slumped down in the chair and started to pass out. "Just tell us once and for all, did you murder Martha and Rebecca?" Alan asked, his patience worn thin. Philip started to laugh, "You are one stupid lawman… yes I killed them. That old bitch wouldn't sell and she was going to let her daughter divorce my useless brother. I was going to pay her far more than the land was worth, but she wanted some hillbilly and his brother to work the land for her… Old bitch told me to leave her house… I got so angry… I didn't realize what I did until it was too late…"

Charles walked over to the fireplace to see the family portrait on the mantle. "You kill George also?" Charles asked, trying not to cry.

216

Philip started to pass out again, this time letting go of the rifle long enough for Alan to grab it. "Wake up!" Alan yelled. Philip jumped slightly, his breathing close to that of a panting dog. "Let me rest, I want to rest," Philip said, his speech slurring further. Charles walked back to Philip, "Did you kill George?" Philip coughed but did not answer.

Charles stood right in front of Philip, his hands twitching from anger. He lurched forward and grabbed Philip by his collar, "Answer me! Did you kill George?" Philip started to laugh during his bouts of coughing, "No, but I did send that madman who thought Rebecca was talking to him… One look at that picture and he said she was talking to him, asking him to love her… Maybe I told him George was the one who killed her… maybe I said George was out to kill him also, it was his mind that made the decision, not mine…"

Charles let go of Philip and stepped backward, "You used a lunatic as your henchmen… he may have done the murdering, but George's blood is on your hands." Alan noticed that Philip's breathing was getting shallower and slower, "He's not drunk, I think he took something. What did you take?" Philip looked up to Alan with his eyes only, "I wish I could move right now deputy… I'd rip your ass apart. You caused all of this to happen, you just couldn't leave it alone. Everyone thought Rebecca killed her mother, but you just had to keep digging. I wish that madman had gotten hold of you and your woman." Alan's face turned beet red,

"Listen you son of a bitch, only a weak man would send someone else to fight his battles. You knew where you could find me… but you send a simple minded man to threaten me by threatening my girlfriend…"

Philip tried to laugh but the coughing was getting worse. "You took something so you could weasel out of the trouble you brought upon yourself. What did you take?" Alan asked. "Alan, there is someone pulling up in a wagon," Ken said looking out the window, "What the hell, I think it is Richard Knilge." Charles looked at Alan, "Why would the undertaker be showing up."

Philip coughed then wheezed, "Because I called him. He's here for me." Charles' face turned white, "You did take something. What the hell did you take?" Alan looked around but did not see anything. He picked up the whiskey bottle and smelled it, "Smells like liquor, nothing else. Philip what did you take?" Philip looked up but could no longer talk as a knock came at the door.

Kenneth opened the door to see Richard Knilge standing in his black suit with a red carnation in the lapel. "Mister Kiel called me during the night to say someone had passed away," Richard said in his usual monotone. "Um, it's Philip Kiel. We believe he took something, he is not doing well," Ken said. "Let him in, Philip just passed," Alan said in disbelief.

The men walked into the parlor to see Philip in the chair, his head slumped to the left and white foam coming from his mouth. Charles walked out onto the porch where the men could hear him sob softly. "Dear God… so much pain for this family. Deputy, if you could help me carry him to the wagon…," Richard said. Alan nodded his head in agreement. As the men started to pick up Philip a small glass bottle fell from beside him to the wood floor. "Put him back down," Alan said.

Ken picked up the bottle and read its label, "Mercury Bichloride." Richard exclaimed sharply, "Oh my, that's poison!" Alan took the bottle from Kenneth and examined it. "It's empty, states it held thirty tablets. I have a feeling he took them all," Alan said. "The mercury eats at the body. It's not a swift death but it a sure one," Richard said, "let's get him out to the wagon, this heat will take to him quickly."

Belle walked out onto the porch and stood with Charles while the others placed Philip in the wagon. "He's been suffering a long time Mister Kiel," Belle said, "I'm sorry, but I listened to your conversation. I never knew he would hurt people… Sir if I knew I would have told someone… I feel responsible." Charles choked back tears, "No Belle if anyone is responsible for his actions it's me. I must have failed him as a father. May God have mercy on his soul."

Ken and Alan walked back to the porch as Richard left with Philip's body. "I guess this puts everything to rest. I will call the sheriff once Ken fixes the wire he cut," Alan said in an official tone. Ken looked over to Alan only to roll his eyes. "Deputy, um, Alan, I am very sorry for the way I treated you this past month or so. I never thought George would kill his wife and I was right, but I also never thought any of my children would commit murder," Charles said in a sad, somber tone. Alan listened to what the proud father had to say, "I do not think any of us could have imaged what would happen. I am just glad it is over. Hopefully he will find himself in a better place."

Henry walked onto the porch, his dirty hat in his hands, "Mister Kiel pass on?" Charles wiped a tear from his cheek, "Yes, just now. You and the others will work for me now. I will take over his property until the courts tells me what to do." Henry slightly shook his head in acknowledgement. "Henry, you never answered my question earlier," Alan said. Henry stood quiet for a second, "Mister Kiel found out that I called on you about the robbery. He said that if I ever talked with you again he…" Henry started to stammer.

"Its fine boy, tell us what he said," Charles stated with compassion. "He said he would… he would do what he wanted with my wife and daughter. I got angry and talked back so he struck me in the face… I sent Julia and Hanna to live with relatives so they would be safe."

220

Charles shook his head in disbelief, "Why did he turn so evil? Is all of this about money and power?" Alan lit a cigarette and took a few puffs, "The man had no soul. Only a soulless man could be this cold and evil… Um, I'm sorry Charles, I should have not have said that." Charles shook his head in disagreement, "No, he was evil. Only an evil man would hurt women. If any good came out of this, it is that George is with Melissa. When she died so did his soul, his body just didn't know to stop." Alan took another last puff of his cigarette then said, "Why don't we take you home Charles."

Chapter 18

Two months have passed since Philip Kiel took his life. The gossip of his death swirled around the town for weeks but has largely died down now. Charles took over his son's property and the Vogal farm as well making him not just the largest land owner in Park County, but also the state of Illinois. While he does not advertise his new title, he does take pride in it. Neither Alan nor Kenneth have talked with Charles often, but when he sees them, he does give a pleasant hello.

Philip was not buried in the family crypt, but under an oak tree on his former property. Olivia did not come to the funeral nor did his daughters. Pastor Crawford said a few words while Charles and Belle said good-bye. A simple wooden cross was placed on the plot, but his name is absent from it. On the same day Philip was entombed, at the potter's field section of the Zion Hill Cemetery in Glasford, Rene was laid to rest. No one came, no words were said and the only mark he made on the earth was a mound of clay.

States Attorney Lange is in the battle of his life to win reelection. Somehow it became knowledge that with Mister Lange, justice can be bought and sold. His opponent capitalized on the rumor and is running on the platform of legal integrity with strict adherence to the word of law; Sheriff Bonner has given his full support. Judging by the talk of the old farmers drinking coffee in the restaurant, Lange will no longer be in office.

As the days past, the corn turned to a dirty yellowish brown and is now wilting in the cool fall air. Alan was driving his REO down the dusty road toward the Lynch farm as the sun was falling toward the horizon at an expedited speed. When he came to the former Vogal farm Alan stopped the car. Where once the burned-out foundation stood, a new house is now under construction. Alan smiled as he looked at it for a second or two before he turned into the driveway leading him to Lynch homestead.

The car came to a screeching stop next to the house where Amie and Robin were sitting on the porch snapping green beans. "Green beans… delicious…," Alan said stepping out of the automobile while trying to hide his dislike for them. "Mom knows how much you love them," Amie said with a smile "Love, oh yes," Alan said. Robin laughed at the faces Alan made. "I see someone is building a new house," Alan said. "Yep, don't know who. I kept badgering pa to find out, but he is too busy with the harvest," Amie said as she snapped the last of the green beans.

"Let's go over there and look at it," Alan said in a persuasive tone. "I don't know, whoever is building it might not want us on their land," Amie said reluctantly. "I'm the deputy, they will not have any objection to a well-known lawman…," Alan said with arrogance and a touch of humor. "Can you take these into mom, please?" Amie asked of Robin. "Sure, I have nothing better to do…," Robin said with displeasure. Alan took Amie's hand and led her off of the porch and down the grassy hill. "Slow down, you're running like a schoolboy!" Amie laughed.

They crossed the road and walked into the yard that was now nothing but trampled weeds and pieces of wood. The smell of pine was strong from the piles of lumber waiting to be placed in the structure. "Doesn't that smell good?" Alan asked. "What, the wood?" Amie asked with a queer face. "Yes! Nothing smells as good as fresh lumber," Alan said with excitement. "Nothing smells better?" Amie asked with a smirk. "Nothing smells as good as you, Honey," Alan said as he wrapped his arms around her waist and then kissed her gently. "Come on, let's go inside!" Alan said with great excitement. Amie just shook her head in disbelief as she walked up a plank into the house almost being tugged along by the grown-up child.

The first floor walls were built and the joists for the second floor were in place. A cool breeze blew through the openings that will soon hold the windows and doors. "It's getting chilly already," Amie said as she made a shivering sound. "Come on, let's sit near the fireplace," Alan said with a smile and gestured off to the right. They walked into what will be the parlor where in the exterior wall was the beginning of a brick fireplace. "Imagine there is a roaring fire keeping us warm," Alan said softly.

224

Amie pulled in closer to him, "It feels nice... maybe we could pop some corn?" Alan pointed to the front of the room, "It looks like it will have nice large windows looking out to the porch and the front yard. Come one, let's go up the stairs!" Amie was comfortable in Alan's arms, but she was picked up and set on her feet by Alan's excitement.

Amie could barely keep up with Alan who seemed to have the fascination of a five year old. They topped the temporary stairs to come onto the second story landing. "I guess we cannot go too far, unless you want to walk on the joists...," Alan said with a wink. "Um, no, not really," Amie said. Alan held his hand out, "Look over there will be the master bedroom and there a smaller bedroom. Over there another bedroom and there... there will be a bathroom!" Amie laughed, "You act as if you saw the plans for the house!"

Alan turned to Amie and took her in his arms, "I have." Amie gave an odd look, "What do you mean?" Alan smiled, "I have seen the plans." Amie shook her head, "You saw the plans, so who is building the house?" Alan gave an innocent look, "I am... for us." Amie pulled back, but was swiftly stopped from falling down the stairs by Alan's quick reflex, "Who for who?" Alan smiled, "Let's go back downstairs before you fall and hurt yourself."

They went down the stairs and walked back out into the yard. "You're building the house?" Amie asked with wide eyes. "Yes, for us," Alan said proudly, "Charles Kiel sold me the home site and ten acres of land for ten dollars. He wanted to pay us back for all the… well, the hell we went through because of his son." Amie gave a small smile while a single tear steamed down her face. "The house will look like the old one, but it will be totally modern; cast iron plumbing, knob and tube wiring and forced air heat with an ample coal bin in the basement," Alan said with the pride of salesman. Amie looked overwhelmed with the news, "Wiring and indoor plumbing? Honey, there's no electricity out here!"

Alan started to laugh, "You act like I don't know that but in two weeks there will be and don't tell you mother, but your parents' house will be hooked up also. Your father and I have been planning all of this without anyone other than Charles and the carpenters knowing about it. Come on to the back yard…" Amie followed Alan as his inner five year old showed again. "I'll fix the barn up; give it a fresh coat of paint. You can have a flower garden over there… maybe a vegetable garden with corn, carrots, potatoes and heck, even green beans! And next spring… right here under this marvelous elm tree we can be married."

Amie cracked a thin smile as the breeze wisped her hair across her face. "Amie I asked your father for permission and I really wanted to ask you in a more romantic place, but I could not keep silent any longer," Alan said as he reached into his shirt pocket. He pulled out a simple gold ring and took

226

Amie's right hand, "Amie I never thought I would meet a woman like you and this past summer proved to me how much I want to enjoy my life with you. Amie will you marry me?" Amie smiled but did not say a word. Alan lost his smile as Amie made him wait for her decision. "Yes," Amie said and before she could utter another word Alan let out a cheer to rival any man.

Alan grabbed Amie into his arms and kissed her in a way that she has never been kissed before. The house may not be finished and they may not be married yet, but Alan felt at that moment he was where he wanted to be in life. Amie placed her head on Alan's chest as he held her tight. "You said you bought ten acres of land also, what will you do with it?" Amie asked. "Your father will show me how to farm… I will always be a deputy, but I like the idea of having my own farm. It may not be much land, but it's enough for us to start with," Alan said, "come on, we better get to the house before your father and his workers eat everything up." Amie wiped the tears of joy from her eyes as she laughed.

"Can I choose the colors?" Amie asked as they walked back to the front yard. "Sure for the paint and tile in the bathroom. I already ordered the bathroom fixtures from Sears and Roebuck; a porcelain pedestal sink, a cast iron tub with brass feet and a high tanked water closet. They should be here next week," Alan said. "Indoor plumbing… I never thought I would have indoor plumbing," Amie said with a trance like tone. "How about electricity? No more oil lamps and you will have modern electrical appliances like…," Alan thought for a moment to his electric hot plate, "well modern appliances."

They came up to the porch just as Grace was calling the men for dinner. Inside the Lynch house Alan saw what dinner looks like at harvest time. The kitchen table was in the dining room with the formal dining table to give extra places to eat. Kenneth hired five men to help with the harvest, the most he ever needed. Everyone found a place to sit with the hired hands at the kitchen table. At the formal dining table Kenneth was at the far end and Grace at the opposite, Robin was to his left with Alan and Amie at the right.

They said Grace then ate a feast of roast chickens, mashed potatoes, green beans, sweetcorn and buttermilk biscuits. It was not until the hired hands left to get well needed rest that Amie announced her engagement to Alan. Grace cried, Kenneth congratulated and Robin smiled but felt left out. When Grace and Robin went to clear the table and Kenneth went to take a smoke on the kitchen porch, the newly engaged couple retired to the cool autumn air of the front porch.

Amie sat on Alan's lap as he held her tightly in his arms. "The house will be ready in the spring, just in time for our wedding," Alan whispered into her ear. "If the events of this summer did not happen, would you still want to marry me?" Amie asked with curiosity. Alan thought very carefully before he answered, "I love you greatly and I always hoped one day you would become my bride. But I will be honest that the lives of the Kiel's taught me that life is far too short. They also taught me that without love we are just souls looking to be loved." Amie closed her eyes and let herself relax in Alan's arms. "Did they teach you anything else?" Amie asked. "Yes," Alan said softly, "I'm glad I don't give up easily."

~ The End ~

www.ingramcontent.com/pod-product-compliance
Lightning Source LLC
Chambersburg PA
CBHW060915180626
46817CB00004B/1271